UPSTAGED

UPSTAGED

Patricia McCowan

ORCA BOOK PUBLISHERS

Library and Archives Canada Cataloguing in Publication

McCowan, Patricia, author
Upstaged / Patricia McCowan.
(Orca limelights)

Issued in print and electronic formats.
ISBN 978-1-4598-1004-4 (paperback).—ISBN 978-1-4598-1005-1 (pdf).—
ISBN 978-1-4598-1006-8 (epub)

I. Title. II. Series: Orca limelights
PS8625.C69U67 2016   jc813'.6   C2015-904522-3

First published in the United States, 2016
Library of Congress Control Number: 2015946190

Summary: In this novel for teens, Ellie loves musical theater and is used to
getting leading roles, but after she moves to the big city, she has to share a
part with a talented girl who seems determined to outshine her.

MIX
Paper from
responsible sources
FSC® C016245

*Orca Book Publishers is dedicated to preserving the environment and has
printed this book on Forest Stewardship Council® certified paper.*

Orca Book Publishers gratefully acknowledges the support for
its publishing programs provided by the following agencies:
the Government of Canada through the Canada Book Fund and the
Canada Council for the Arts, and the Province of British Columbia
through the BC Arts Council and the Book Publishing Tax Credit.

Cover design by Rachel Page
Cover photography by Corbis

ORCA BOOK PUBLISHERS
www.orcabook.com

Printed and bound in Canada.

19 18 17 16 • 4 3 2 1

To my arts-loving daughters.

One

nce again, I do the only thing that's made my school mornings bearable for the last week. Still in bed, I haul my laptop off the floor, go to the bookmarked site, click *Play* and settle in. There I am, center stage, belting out "Popular" from the Rossmere Heights School production of *Wicked*. The spotlight follows me as I sing about all of the ways I'll make over Elphaba, played by my best friend, Cassidy. It was last June, only three months ago. Forever ago. I start to sing along. My cell phone buzzes on the bedside table.

"Yes, Dad, I'm getting ready for school," I say before he can get a word in. I mute the video but keep watching. "Shouldn't you be chatting up some local hotshot right now?"

"That's why I'm calling, Ellie." Dad's voice is way too chipper for eight in the morning. "Watch the next guest. I think you'll be interested."

Dad's the new host on the local TV show *This City This Morning*. It's been a month now. A month since he dragged me away from Rossmere Heights to come to Toronto. Where my new high school doesn't even have a drama club. Band, debating, coding and even archery, yes. Drama, no.

"It's not another *social media's eating your teen's brain* story, is it?"

Dad sighs. "No. Just watch it, okay? I have to go. Love you."

"Back at you." Though I'd love him more if he hadn't messed up my life so much.

I close my laptop, drag myself out of bed and pad out to the condo living room. Even after a month, I'm still freaked by the floor-to-ceiling windows in here. Our high-up view is cluttered with the windows of other buildings. Other buildings filled with other people. I'm all for an audience, just not in my own living room. I slouch down onto the still-smells-new sectional and swap my cell for the TV remote.

"Welcome back. It's five past eight," Dad says from the tall stool he's told me is too slippery. He's six-foot-one and not really made for perching. A woman with short black hair smiles from the stool beside him. She *is* made for perching. She's petite and curvy, rocking a tight red dress and matching lipstick.

"In our studio with me now is Renée Felix, artistic director of the Youth Works Theater Company, or YWTC, for short. She is a passionate believer in the power of musical theater to engage youth."

I sit up straighter.

"Good morning, Mike." Her voice is melted-butter smooth.

"You know, Renée"—Dad smiles at her, then at the camera—"some of our viewers may not believe this, but I once trod the boards myself. Back in high school. In *The Boyfriend*."

I moan. "Your viewers don't want to know."

"I'll bet you were the boyfriend," Renée says, right on cue.

"How did you guess?" He laughs and points off-camera. "Okay, my producer is now spitting out her coffee, so we better move on."

Renée feigns disappointment. "You're not going to sing for us?"

"Better not. Tell us about YWTC."

"Please!" I say.

"We mount top-notch musical-theater productions, in a professional theater, entirely with actors aged thirteen to nineteen." Renée delivers this mission statement with a warmth that makes it sound like a fancy French meal. And I'm hungry for it. "I hire professional directors and choreographers, so each rehearsal process is like a master class in musical theater for our performers."

"Wow." Dad pulls his head back. "Sounds intense. But exciting too."

Always the cheerleader. Breakfast television is not exactly hard-hitting journalism.

"They love it, Mike. It is such a learning experience, to see what it takes to put together a show. They really bond working together. And, of course, it's fun too. It is musical theater, after all!"

"Absolutely. And where do you find these performers, Renée?" Dad turns toward the camera. Toward me.

"Yes, Dad, I'm getting this," I answer back. He's been on my case about moping around the condo too much. And I've been helping him feel guilty about having to leave Rossmere Heights. Could this theater company be the one thing that doesn't suck about moving here?

"Mike, you know this city is such a theater town." Renée touches his arm. "It's filled with teens who have grown up seeing wonderful shows—*The Phantom of the Opera, Legally Blonde, Mama Mia!* They're keen for the chance to discover what it's like to actually be in one. We have a lot of interest."

Filled with teens. I picture gangs of musical-theater nerds dancing their way around the subway, breaking into song. I wish.

"And you're going to be giving those teens that chance again soon, isn't that right?" Dad glances off-camera. Probably getting the "keep-things-moving" signal from Bev, his producer.

"Our next show is in late November, so we start rehearsals September 25th. We're holding auditions for it this Saturday and Sunday at the East End United Church. Our website has all the details."

"Yes, we've got that address on the bottom of your screen," Dad interjects, looking at the camera.

I grab a pen off the coffee table and write the website address on the back of my hand. It's shaky. The word *auditions* has made me nervous.

Dad turns back to Renée. "What's the show? Something classic? Like *The Boyfriend*?" He winks.

I throw the pen at the TV. "Enough with *The Boyfriend*."

"No, something new," Renée says, ignoring the bait. "We're very excited. It's a new off-Broadway musical called *Schooled*. The storyline is perfect for teen actors. It takes place in a boarding school. Sort of a mash-up between *Annie* and *Hairspray*."

"That sounds weird." I slump back into the couch.

"Sounds great," Dad says, clearly having no clue what such a show would look like. He smiles at Renée and then at the camera. "Okay, future musical-theater stars, polish up your best songs and—"

I turn off the TV. I stare at the address on my hand but don't move to get my laptop. The condo is silent all around me.

I never had to audition at my school. I was Sandy in *Grease*, Dorothy in *The Wizard of Oz*,

Galinda in *Wicked*, because our drama and choir teacher, Mrs. Mowat, knew I was the best one for the lead roles.

And what about all of those musical-theater-savvy kids Renée Felix mentioned? How many of them would I be up against in an audition?

My phone buzzes on the coffee table. Dad's text reads, **Told you you'd be interested! :)**

I don't text back. But the phone's clock tells me I'm going to be late for school. Again. I look over to the wall of windows and wish for the thousandth time that I'd never had to leave Rossmere Heights, where I knew I always had a place onstage. I yank my pajama sleeves down, covering up the writing on my hand.

Two

L eaving school alone at three thirty, I get hit full-on by one of those warm September afternoons that make you curse the inventor of school. All around me, kids busily thumb their phones. The Java Jones across the street is already lined up out the door.

I take off my hoodie as I walk, hoping to absorb some sunshiny happiness. This is the sort of afternoon when Cassidy and the other drama kids and I would raid the chips aisle at the Kwik Mart and head down to Clarey Park by the river. We'd gossip and do fake music videos around the picnic benches and weeping-willow trees.

A jolt of missing Cassidy makes me stop on the spot. I pull out my phone and text her. **Hey, homegirl! School out?** A streetcar turns the corner, the metal-on-metal squeal of its wheels piercing my head.

Yep.

Knowing she's there on the other end of the phone makes me smile. I lean against the corner of a bank building, ignoring the people streaming past. **Home in 10. Skype time?**

Can't. Sorry. :(1st meeting for West Side Story 2day! Rehearsals start nxt wk. :D

I let my backpack slump to the ground. *West Side Story?!*

Didn't I tell you?

She didn't. I'd have remembered. It's my favorite old-school musical. As Cassidy knows. **Forgot. Been busy!** I lie.

Glam big-city life! Hoping for Maria. Gotta go now.

Maria. The lead. If I were still there, that role would be mine.

My phone vibrates in my hand, a nudge. **Wish me luck!!**

Luck, I text back.

Bye-bye sunshiny happiness. I pocket my phone and start walking again. I get to the condo building, pull open the smoke-gray glass door and trudge through the lobby. I hit the elevator button and suddenly can't wait to get upstairs. Not to watch the Rossmere Heights production of *Wicked* again, but to get an audition time for the Youth Works Theater Company. Maybe I can't be Maria, but perhaps I can at least get myself back onstage.

The elevator doors open with a chime. The first note of a new song.

* * *

Audition day. After riding the subway past two stops before realizing I was going west, not east, getting onto the train going east and then running the block and a half from my stop to the East End United Church, I'm sweaty and short of breath. I yank open the ancient door, and it's so dark inside I can barely see.

"Are you here for the *Schooled* auditions?" a sharp voice asks. My eyes adjust. At the end of a short hallway, a young woman sits behind a table next to a closed door.

"I am." I hurry over. "My name's Ellie Fisk."

Now that I'm closer, I can see she's probably nineteen or twenty. Her thick black hair is short, with purple streaks through it. Her nose is pierced with a tiny purple gem.

"Fist?" She frowns at her laptop.

"Fisk."

A sign on the table reads *Audition in Progress. Quiet, Please!* I can hear a male voice singing from behind the door. "Miracle of Miracles" from *Fiddler on the Roof.* He sounds fantastic.

As the girl at the table works the touchpad with one hand, her other one snakes out to a plastic bag filled with gummy bears. She pops two into her mouth, does a final click and looks up. I smile. She doesn't.

"I'm Neeta Patel, the stage manager," she says, brisk and businesslike despite the gummies. "We've had a ridiculous number of people auditioning, so things are running a smidge late. Makes me insane. You're the last one today, hallelujah. Have a seat. You're after Marissa Ivan." She points over to a bench I hadn't noticed, where a girl my age sits studying a binder on her lap.

"Thanks."

Neeta nods, pops another gummy and goes back to her screen.

I sit. The girl on the bench flips through the pages in her binder, her straight brown hair half blocking my view of her face.

"Hi, I'm Ellie." I keep my voice low but friendly.

She glances over, flicks her bangs away from her eyes. "Marissa."

"I've never auditioned for this company before. You?"

"I've been with YWTC for three years." Her eyes give me a quick once-over. "Can we not talk? I like to focus before an audition." Though she barely opens her mouth, I notice big white teeth. *All the better to snap at you with, my dear.*

"Oh. Sure." Three years. I wonder what sort of roles she's had, how good she is. I pull my sheet music out of my bag and look over it one last time.

A burst of angry monologue—"I told you not to mess with Carlos!"—comes from the audition room, startling me.

"Yikes. Sounds serious," I joke.

Marissa keeps reading. Neeta keeps chewing.

I sit there, butt on a hard pew, back against a hard plaster wall. Is everyone in YWTC so grim? Where's the musical-theater happiness? Where's the feeling that everyone could break into song because life is so gosh-darn swell? If Neeta and Marissa are typical of the theater-loving young people that Renée Felix cooed about on my dad's show, I'd hate to meet the theater-hating ones.

The door to the audition room opens, and a slim guy with curly, brown hair struts out. "Nailed it."

Neeta snorts but smiles.

The guy points both hands, pistol-style, at Marissa. "Your turn, Ivan the Terrible."

Ivan the Terrible? I look sideways at Marissa, half-worried she'll pull a real gun on the guy, but she laughs as she and her binder head into the audition room. "Camilla! Great to see you again. How was New York?" she says before the door closes.

I guess it's just me who gets the cold shoulder.

"Omigod, look at you!" Nailed-it guy is staring at me, hand on his chest.

"What?" I stand up to check myself out. Was I sitting in something? Sweating through my shirt?

"You look like Snow White, all black-haired, blue-eyed, lost-in-the-woods goodness," he says in a tone of wonder.

I laugh, surprised and relieved. "No one has ever told me *that* before."

Neeta shushes us. "You're scaring the poor girl."

He shields his mouth from her and stage-whispers, "Sorry."

"Actually," I whisper back, "you're the first person here who hasn't scared me."

He nods. "Neeta and Marissa can be a tad sharp." He thrusts out his hand. "Gregor."

We shake. "Ellie."

Marissa's singing cuts through our conversation with the opening bars from "Popular."

I drop back down on the bench. "Oh no."

"Oh no is right." Gregor joins me. "Marissa should know better. That song is so overdone."

"It is?"

"Totally. Because it makes every person who sings it feel sassy and bossy in a cute way, which is not how anyone feels at an audition, right? So it's an ego boost. But it must be pretty annoying for directors to listen to, over and over." He rattles this off like an expert.

I start to sweat again. "It's the song I was going to sing."

Gregor smacks his forehead. "As you can tell, I've written a book called *How to Not Make Friends in Five Minutes.*"

I'd laugh, except I have a blooming sense that I should forget this whole audition idea.

Gregor must see my panic. He turns to face me full-on. "But seriously, do yourself a favor and sing something else. What other songs did you bring?"

"This is it." I hold up my flimsy pages of sheet music. I had been so proud of myself last night, finding it online, buying and printing a copy, going over it a bit. I realize now what must have been in Marissa's binder: a massive collection of songs she's practiced to perfection.

"You brought one song?" Gregor's delivery conveys half disbelief, half pity.

"Stupid, right?"

He waves that aside. "Anything you know by heart?"

I think of the songs I sang at Rossmere Heights. "'Somewhere Over the Rainbow'?"

"Nope. Overdone, too slow, the high notes flatten if you're nervous."

"'Hopelessly Devoted to You'?"

Gregor grips my forearm gently. "Girlfriend, you will be if I can help you out here, but no. You're not Olivia Newton-John-y enough."

I can hear Marissa speaking now. She's on her monologue. My turn's coming fast. "The only other stuff I'm good at is from *Annie*. And that's too young. I did it in sixth grade."

Gregor hoots. "I love it. I did 'Tomorrow' for my first YWTC audition four years ago."

"You sang Annie?" Now I'm confused as well as panicked.

"Before my voice changed, of course. It was my homage to Sarah Jessica Parker." He makes jazz hands up beside his face.

"Nothing you say is making sense." I resist the urge to grab his jazz hands.

He gasps, widening his already large eyes. "S.J.P. played Annie on Broadway when she was a sprout. How can you be into musical theater and not know that?"

I'm starting to feel like there's a lot I don't know. Marissa exits the audition room. She beams but keeps her eyes down, like she's carrying a fantastic secret.

Neeta says, "Ellie, you're up."

I'm frozen to the spot.

Gregor pulls me off the bench. "Come on, little Orphan Annie. I'll be your accompanist."

"But I don't have the music for you to play."

"It's all in here." He points at his temple. "And I'm an exceptional pianist. Because yes, I'm that brilliant."

Marissa darts a narrow look at me as Gregor and I go by. Neeta says, "Hey, Gregor!"

"It's an emergency," he says.

And then I'm in the bright, overly warm audition room. Renée Felix and two other people face me from behind a long table littered with papers and coffee cups. A thirtysomething guy with thick-framed glasses and a beard says, "Welcome. I'm Drew Carrier, the director and musical director of *Schooled.* What are you going to sing for us today?"

Three

'm singing "Tomorrow" for three strangers. My voice vibrates in my chest, in my head. I stick out my chin when the song tells me to. I grin. It's hard to grin and sing. Behind the table, Drew Carrier leans forward on his elbows. The leggy choreographer—she was introduced, but I've already forgotten her name—squints. Am I hurting her ears? Renée Felix reclines away from the other two, looking artistic director-ish.

On my next quick breath, I glance to my right, to Gregor at the piano. He's cheery and attentive for cues. Sandy the dog to my Annie.

I forgot how quickly "Tomorrow" goes by. But at least I've remembered the words.

I take a huge breath to propel into the song's wide-open, optimistic finish. I hit the last big note bang-on and hold it—"*aaa-waaaayy*"—then wrap it up with what I hope is my best downtrodden-but-still-hopeful expression: *You have to adopt me. I'm adorable!* Gregor's hands spring off the keyboard in a final flourish. I can practically hear the applause.

Except there is none.

Drew pushes his glasses up on his nose. "Charming."

"Isn't she?" Gregor pipes up. "I found her outside. Can we keep her?"

Renée laughs. The choreographer smiles—barely. *Camilla Perez.* Her name pops back into my head now that there's space for it.

Drew chuckles. "Gregor, I know this will be hard for you, but it's time to shut up and leave so that..." He shuffles through the papers in front of him.

"Ellie," I prompt.

"So that Ellie can do her monologue." Drew raises a thick eyebrow at me. "Gregor can be a merciless upstager."

"Hey!" Gregor pretends to look offended. "Only amateurs upstage. I simply have charisma. But I can mute it." He makes a zip-it gesture on his mouth.

It was less scary doing my song with him in the room. Maybe he'll be good for my monologue too. "He can stay. I don't mind."

Gregor mimes clapping.

Renée shakes her head at me. "No, dear, that's not professional." She's pleasant but firm. "He's a fellow auditioner. It was unusual enough to let him accompany you." She slides her eyes toward Drew.

"It gave me a break from having to accompany everyone," he says, shrugging. "But, of course, you're right."

Gregor throws up his hands and pushes away from the piano. "I surrender. I'm going."

"Thanks for your playing," I say as he passes behind me. "It was great."

"Anytime, Snow White. And I know."

I watch the door close behind him, then turn back to the table of judges.

"Let's hear what you've got." Drew clasps his hands behind his head, settling in to listen.

"I'll be doing Mimi from *Oranges and Lemons.*" In drama last year, Mrs. Mowat said I was so good at this it gave her shivers.

"An old classic." Drew nods.

Hoping classic is good, I look at the floor for a second and take a settling breath. I lift my head, look right at Drew and begin. "It's not like we knew the truth, Oscar and me. Mama kept the news from us until it was too late. So we shouldn't be blamed for...for what happened last night."

Drew suddenly leans forward. "Okay. Let's stop there, Ellie."

I feel my mouth snap shut. Stop? Is my audition over? What could I have done wrong in thirty seconds? I glance at Renée. Her face gives nothing away.

"What do you think Mimi wants?" Drew asks. His tone is friendly, but my heart is skittering against my ribs.

"Wants?"

"What does she want to achieve by saying those lines?"

My hands feel sweaty. I don't want to rub them on my jeans and look dorky and nervous. I settle for putting them on my hips. "Mimi wants to achieve...uh, I think she's saying, to Papa—"

"Good. You know who she's talking to. Monologues aren't addressed to the air. Or to the people you're auditioning in front of. Are they?"

21

Oh crap, I shouldn't have stared at Drew. "No."

"They're addressed to someone specific."

"Right." Someone specifically not the director.

"So. Mimi." Drew rolls up the sleeves of his plaid shirt. "What are you hoping Papa thinks when you tell him what you and Oscar did?"

I'm hoping Drew thinks I have enough of a brain to cast me in a lead role. But I try to put myself in Mimi's place. "That it wasn't our fault. I mean, it *was* our fault, but Mimi—I want Papa to think it wasn't. So that Oscar and I won't get sent away. I don't want to be sent away."

"Yes!" Drew hits the tabletop. "High stakes. Do it again with that in mind."

Camilla stretches her neck from side to side. I remember that I'm the last person to audition today. They all must want to be done.

I straighten my shoulders and start the monologue again, without staring at Drew. I focus on a spot slightly above him and conjure in my head an image of Papa, suspicious and distrustful. Drew doesn't interrupt this time. I even feel myself tear up toward the end and have to swallow hard before my final line: "*Papa, please tell me you understand.*"

Silence.

I take a step back, as if leaving Mimi, then look at Drew. I'm pulsing. Just like Gregor declared when he came out of his audition, I nailed it.

Camilla gives Drew a *Well?* look.

"Nice," he says.

That's it? *Nice* doesn't land the big role. When Drew doesn't go on, I have to fill the silence. "Thank you. That was a really interesting audition. I mean, you made it interesting. For me." I wish Gregor could come back to play some exit music.

Camilla picks my résumé off the table and scans it. "I see you have no dance background, Ellie." Her voice is sweet yet somehow hard. Crunchy candy.

I want to shout, *Did you not just hear me sing? Did you not just see me act?* But I keep positive. "I was Dorothy in *The Wizard of Oz* and Sandy in *Grease*, and in *Wicked* I played Galinda, so I danced in all of those. All the solos and most of the other numbers."

"Those aren't dance-heavy shows." Camilla folds herself into a cross-legged position on her chair. "Have you taken any classes outside of school? Some basic ballet, maybe?"

I decide to try some humor. "The only dance school in my old town was in the mall attached to the main grocery store. Not very glamorous. And the woman who ran it was this scary ex-Soviet ballerina, so I was afraid to go."

Camilla grimaces and tilts her head. "So, no?"

Bye-bye humor. "No."

"Okay," she says, like it's not okay.

Drew clears his throat. "Nicely done, Ellie." He gathers up his notes and taps them into a pile, newscaster style.

Renée stands and smooths her plum-colored skirt down her hips. "Thanks for trying out, Ellie. It's going to be an exciting show. Now Drew and Camilla need to put their heads together to see who gets callbacks."

"That's when the dance audition happens," Camilla says. In case I'm too dumb to figure out that she only gives the people who might be cast a chance to prove they can dance. Or not.

Drew says, "We'll be in touch later tonight to let everyone know one way or the other."

I've tanked the audition.

"Thanks so much," I manage to say, then bolt from the room.

Gregor's gone. Neeta looks up from her laptop, snaps it shut and makes a beeline for the audition room. "Thanks for auditioning. They'll let you know," she says, brushing past.

One way or the other.

I'll be other.

Four

slump in front of the TV, alone with a bowl of reheated pasta. Dad's stuck in a work dinner with his boss. *American Idol* plays a mash-up of the season's worst auditions—the deluded, tone-deaf people who get eliminated three bars into their songs. I turn it off. This is a lousy way to shake off my post-audition unhappiness.

I go to the kitchen and dump out what's left of my pasta. My cell buzzes from the coffee table. It'll be Drew, telling me I'm not getting a callback. Don't pick it up, I tell myself. Pretend the audition didn't happen. The phone keeps vibrating, like a trapped wasp. I stare at it until it goes still.

Good. That's the end of that stupid idea. I'm not ready for the Youth Works Theater Company. I grab an apple from the fridge.

Just as I take a bite, my phone starts up again. I chew, swallow. There's no avoiding the truth, I guess. I pick up the phone without looking at it.

"Hello?" I try to sound calm and mature.

"Ellie?"

"Cassidy?"

"You're there! Thank goodness, because if I couldn't tell you right this minute I'd explode." Her voice is high-pitched with excitement. "I got Maria! Can you believe it? I mean, I sort of knew I would, but I sort of worried I wouldn't. And omigod, Jared's playing Tony. He said he's even going to dye his hair black for the part. Won't he look even hotter than he already does? I am so, so happy he and I are going to be the leads."

I sink onto the couch. "Wow. That's awesome, Cass." The chunk of apple sits like a rock in my stomach. "Congrats."

"Thanks." Silence. Maybe she's finally taking a breath. "I wish you were still here." She's quieter. "Guess where I'm calling from."

Against my will, I smile. "Top bleacher by first base." The baseball diamond is where Cassidy and I have always gone to share our most important secrets or news, even in the middle of winter.

"I knew you'd know. And that weirdo from the apartment on the corner still lets his basset hound poop in center field. It's circling as I speak."

I laugh, but if I hear too much about my old neighborhood right now, I'll probably cry. "So when do you start rehearsals?" Not that I really want to hear about that either.

"Day after tomorrow. I'm so excited. Except Tessa Gorsham's playing Anita. Talk about miscasting. She's about as fiery as a dictionary." Cassidy's back in high-pitched babble mode. My cue to cut things short.

"Cass, my dad's just walked in, I should go." I go over and open our balcony door to make a fake, Dad-coming-in sound.

"Hi, Mr. Fisk!" Cassidy calls. "Okay, talk soon."

"Yep."

"I miss you. Bye." If her voice gets any higher, it'll crack my phone.

I press *End*.

She didn't ask me a single thing about what's going on in my life. Just as well.

I realize I'm staring off into space only when a movement catches my eye. On a balcony across the way, a guy waves an oven mitt over a smoky barbecue. He looks up, smiles and waves the mitt at me. "I'm such an amateur," he shouts cheerfully. I slide the door shut. I've pulled the blind down halfway when my phone buzzes again. For a brief, weird second I think the balcony guy has somehow figured out my phone number. Then I remember who it probably is.

I clear my throat. "Hello?"

"Is this Ellie Fisk?" Drew asks. His voice sounds younger on the phone.

"Speaking." I wonder how many calls he's made today. How many people he's disappointed.

"You did a great job at the audition. We'd like to see you at the callback. Tomorrow at three o'clock, at the church. I hope you're available."

Air rushes into my lungs. I dance on the spot and let out a silent scream. Then I calm myself down enough to say, "Totally. I am totally available. One hundred percent available." Maybe not so calm.

Drew laughs. "Good to know. Bring jazz shoes, if you've got them, and wear stuff you can move easily in. Camilla will teach everyone a routine. The dance audition is a group thing."

"Great." Thank goodness I don't have to be in a room alone with her.

"See you tomorrow," Drew says. "One hundred percent, right?"

"Exactly."

I let happiness settle over me. I did not tank my first real audition ever. I did *a great job*. I grab my apple and my laptop. Time to find a place to buy some lucky jazz shoes, pronto.

* * *

"Kick ball change, kick ball change, chaîné, and chaîné, and—no, no, you've got to keep the spacing even between dancers. Allie"—Camilla points at me—"pick up your turns. You were too far behind Marissa."

It would be nice if Camilla actually got my name right. But I guess it would also be nice if I had known that a chaîné was a type of turn before she started yelling the word at me. Marissa casually practices the combo I just messed up.

Drew, at the piano, says, "Where should we take it from?"

"From the grapevine, everyone." Camilla snaps her fingers to make us hurry.

The five other kids and I scurry back to our original spots. We're the first group to do the dance. Twenty-three additional would-be cast members sprawl on the audition-room floor in front of us. They're stretching and warming up, but they're also watching our every move. Learning from any mistakes.

Camilla smacks her rock-hard thigh as she counts, "And one and two and..."

Drew starts up on the piano again.

I say the steps in my head, making sure not to move my lips at the same time.

"Keep smiling," Camilla shouts. "It's not a death march. Yet."

I smile. On the second chaîné, I glance over to make sure I'm close enough to Marissa.

"Heads up." Camilla slaps the bottom of her chin to demonstrate. "Better. Final turn, and land it."

Drew hits the last chord. Yes! That time felt solid. I'm hoping the next group of six will get called up so I can be done. My new jazz shoes are killing me.

"Once more, just to see if you can get it right twice in a row," Camilla says.

Moving back into position, I catch Gregor, out on the floor, sighing loudly. He says something to the tall black girl beside him. She laughs and hits him playfully on the arm, the way good friends can. Am I the only person here who doesn't know anyone?

"And one and two and," Camilla calls again.

I'm grapevining, I'm kick ball changing, kick ball changing, I'm smiling, I'm chaîné-ing, heads up, I'm—

I bash into Marissa. "Omigod, I'm sorry."

She hasn't fallen but only because she's grabbed on to the dancer beside her for balance.

"Are you okay, Ilona?" Marissa asks the girl.

Ilona looks miffed but says, "No biggie."

"Sorry," I repeat. Heat spreads up my neck and face, a tide of embarrassment. "I didn't want to be too far from you, but I guess that was too close."

"You think?" Marissa flicks her bangs out of her eyes, then asks Camilla, "From the top again?"

Camilla snaps the waistband of her leggings like a metronome. Maybe that helps her think. "No. This group can leave." She turns to the waiting actors. "Next six up."

Marissa strides away, snatches the water bottle from her dance bag and takes a long drink. She doesn't leave but stands beside an athletic-looking guy near the back of the room and starts whispering furiously. He nods his big blond head in agreement as he stretches his quadriceps.

I change out of my jazz shoes, stuff them in my backpack and hurry toward the exit.

"Hey, Ellie." Gregor leans over as I pass by. "If you can hang around until we're done, Shantel and I are going for coffee and gossip," he says, gesturing to the girl beside him. "You could come with us."

Shantel leans across his legs. "He gossips. I intelligently analyze our fellow actors."

"In other words, you gossip," Gregor says, putting his face beside hers.

"Oh, snap!" Shantel pushes his head away with one finger.

For a second, I want to go and listen to their rapid-fire joking so I can forget about my callback. Then I picture having to watch everyone else be way better dancers than me.

"Thanks," I say. "But my dad's meeting me, so I have to go."

Camilla calls, "Silence, minions!" without turning around.

Shantel and Gregor clamp their hands over their mouths in exaggerated fear. Then he whispers, "Okay, see you at the first rehearsal, Snow."

I doubt it.

Outside, the late-afternoon light is low. There's a chill in the air. Cars drive by, people walk by, the whole busy city goes by. Everybody knows exactly what they're doing and how to get where they're going.

I lied when I said I was meeting Dad, but I decide to change that. I take out my phone.

Dad sounds tired. "Hey, El, just finished at the gym. How was the callback?"

"Have you found a good Chinese food place in this city yet? I need emergency chicken fried rice."

"Hang tight," Dad says. "I'll be there in five."

Five

At the King's Bowl restaurant, our middle-aged waiter's face transforms from bland to excited as he finishes taking our order. "*This City This Morning*!" he announces, like that's Dad's name. "I watch you when I'm getting dressed."

"That's awkward," I say under my breath.

Dad shoots me a look. "Fantastic," he says to the waiter, deploying his best TV smile. "I hope I get your day off to a good start."

"Oh yes. But my wife says the old host was better. Leanne." The waiter furrows his brow as he takes our menus from us. "My wife listens to the radio now."

"Whatever makes her happy, right?" Dad says, smile hanging in there.

The waiter shrugs and leaves us to wait for our food.

"He should divorce his wife," I say.

Dad laughs. "My whole week has been phone calls and emails saying, *I'm so sad Leanne's gone.* Or *Leanne would never mispronounce Roncesvalles Avenue.*"

"That sucks." Dad talked about work the whole time we were in the car, so I don't say anything else in case he keeps going. I shift the soy-sauce bottle around on the table.

"So." Dad takes the bottle out of my hand and sets it aside. "The callback?"

"I don't really want to talk about it." I look past Dad to the big aquarium behind him. A pinky-beige monster fish stares at me with bulgy eyes. Maybe it's better to look back at Dad.

Less bulgy-eyed, but his expression is an old favorite: *Don't even try to pretend with me.* "I didn't drive to your audition to answer an emergency chicken-fried-rice call for nothing."

"Okay." I take a big breath and let it all out. "I'm not ready for this theater company. It's too serious. The choreographer is a drill sergeant.

The director stopped me two seconds into my audition. There's a girl in the cast—"

"Nobody's *in the cast* yet. Everybody's still trying out."

I roll my eyes at him. "She'll be cast, I can tell. And she has an instant hate-on for me. No reason."

"Thank you," Dad says as the waiter plunks down our drinks, then continues once he's gone. "Negative people always stand out. Like all the critics who called me this week. For every one of those, there are probably ten others who think I'm fine but don't bother to call. There have to be some good things about the company, Ellie."

I think about Gregor accompanying me, about Drew telling me I had a good audition. That's great, but...I shrug. "I forgot to tell you. Cassidy got the lead in *West Side Story* at Rossmere."

"Aha." Dad leans back in his chair and considers me. "Good for Cassidy. And you're getting the chance to be in a cool new musical in Toronto because your dad finally got his dream job here."

Mr. Positive is not helping. "Interviewing school principals about fall fairs while strangers watch in their undies is your dream job?"

Dad's smile freezes on the spot.

I'm being a jerk. Before I can apologize, the waiter appears beside the table, our plates of food balanced up his arm. He sets them down in the middle of our silence.

"Thank goodness the food's so fast here," Dad says cheerily. "My daughter's in desperate need of this. Gets grumpy with her dad when she's hungry."

I sip my iced tea to avoid saying anything.

"She's hangry. Hungry and angry!" the waiter declares, thumping Dad's shoulder old-buddy style. "Remember that nutritionist on your show last Friday?" He wags a finger at me. "Don't be hangry to your dad!" He walks away chuckling.

Dad snaps open his napkin and puts it on his lap. "And *that* is why it's my dream job."

"I guess I deserved that," I say, though being hangry feels like the least of my problems.

"Listen." Dad dishes out the chicken fried rice, the sweet-and-sour pork, the wontons. "It's been hard watching you sulk around the condo since we moved here. Youth Works Theater Company sounded like it could be a fun thing. If you don't want to do that, fine. But you do have to find something to do."

I pour the radioactive-red sweet-and-sour sauce over my wontons. "It's not up to me at this point. At least, not about the play. If I don't get in, I don't get in."

"It's up to you to decide to really live here now." He gives me another old-favorite look: *You know I'm right.*

I don't say anything. Because he's the one who decided to move here, and Drew and Camilla are the ones who'll decide if I get into *Schooled.* How can I decide anything if the choices aren't mine?

"Come on, dig in while it's hot," Dad says.

We eat in silence. Except Dad hums while he chews. A goofy habit, it's always meant he's happy. I guess it's good that one of us is.

Behind Dad, the monster fish circles the tank, forcing smaller ones to get out of its way. I privately name it Marissa. Satisfied, I crunch into a wonton.

"Food's good here, hey? Chicken fried rice meets your high standards?" Dad asks. I can tell he's ready to move on, is looking forward to restarting his work week tomorrow.

I nod, but I'm not ready to let him think everything's better. For me, tomorrow means another empty week of school.

Soon the waiter returns. "No more hangry?" he asks me.

I lick the last bit of sweet-and-sour sauce from my fingers. "Nope."

"Good." He puts the bill and a couple of fortune cookies down in front of us. "See you tomorrow, *This City This Morning*," he says to Dad as he whisks our plates away.

"You're right," Dad whispers. "That is a bit awkward."

I laugh. My cell phone buzzes in my bag. I pull it out and check the call display. My stomach fizzes. "Already?"

"Already who?" Dad's cracking into his fortune cookie.

I turn away from him. "Hello?"

"Ellie. Drew Carrier here."

"I know." That sounds rude. I try again. "Hi there." The bustling restaurant noises mute into a quiet fog of focus.

I hear Drew take a sip of something. I picture him at the audition table again, surrounded by notes. "Thanks for doing the callback today."

And knocking another dancer over with your clumsy moves, thus making it easy for me to tell you that we won't be casting you!

"It was fun," I lie.

"I'm glad you thought so. I know Camilla can be intimidating, but you'll find she's an amazing choreographer to work with."

"I...I will?" I look at Dad. He's mouthing, *What? What?* I hold up a finger to make him wait. "You mean...does that mean—"

"I'd like you to be in *Schooled*, Ellie." I hear the smile in Drew's voice. "So do Camilla and Renée. We think you'd do a great job as Piper."

They want me. An angel chorus sings in my head. Except I have no idea who Piper is. But she has a name. That's a good sign. Ensemble characters don't have names. I have to say something. "Wow. Are you sure?" I grimace. Wrong thing to say. "I mean, you decided so fast."

"I work fast. I'd pretty much decided you were a good fit after your first audition. The callback was just to confirm. I like to put a cast together quickly."

"That's great." I stare at Dad, and he stares back, dopey smile probably mirroring mine.

"Now, the role is double cast. You'd be playing Piper on alternate nights with another actor."

"Oh." I feel suspended in midair for a second. "That's okay." I'm still so excited my brain's hardly connecting to my mouth.

"So you'll join us?" Drew asks. "It's a big undertaking—rehearsals are every Friday evening and all day Sunday. They're intense, but YWTC is a terrific company to be part of."

I grip the table so I don't float away. "I'd love to be part of it. Yes."

"Wonderful. I'll email you all the details tonight. Rehearsal schedule, performance schedule. There's a commitment form you'll need to print off and sign and bring to the first rehearsal next Friday."

"Okay. Will do." The week ahead clicks into place. The months ahead. Finally, I can look forward to something.

Dad's unwrapping the second fortune cookie.

"Welcome aboard," Drew says before he hangs up.

I put the phone down and dance my arms in the air. "Yes, yes, yes, yes, yes!"

"Here's to you, Ellie." Dad hands me the cookie. "Open it up. Read it."

I crack it apart. The slip of paper sticks out of one half like a little white tongue. I pause, look at Dad. "I got a role, but it's double cast. I'm sharing it with someone."

He waves that aside. "You're cast. That's all that counts right now."

Excitement bubbles back up in me again. "Right." I pull out the fortune. *If you don't do it excellently, don't do it at all.*

I laugh and slide it across the table to him. "Even the fortune cookies are intense in this city."

But I don't care. I can do excellently. Landing a role in *Schooled* proves it. Even a shared role.

Dad puts his arm around my shoulders as we head toward the door. "Hey," I say. "What was your fortune?"

He pulls it out of his back pocket and reads, "*You learn from mistakes. You learned a lot this week.* Bring on a new week, I say."

I happily agree.

Six

The rehearsal hall knocks the breath out of me. I pause inside the door to take in the high brick walls and wooden floors of the old warehouse space. The late-afternoon sun slants through a row of windows, lighting the table where Drew, Renée and Neeta, the stage manager, talk together. A large circle of chairs faces them. Past the chairs, a short stocky guy plays "On Broadway" on a piano while other kids sing and dance along.

"We're seriously not in Kansas anymore, Toto," I murmur to myself. "This rocks." I snap a photo of the scene with my phone. I don't want to look like some small-town hick, but this will make Cassidy drool.

I'm always excited at first read-throughs, but this one feels extra exciting.

"On Broadway" finishes, the group breaks apart, and I join in their applause. I scan the faces, hoping to see Gregor. There's his friend Shantel, and...ugh. There's Marissa. She leans back and laughs at something said by the big-headed blond guy she hung out with at the callback. I'm not surprised she's in the play. I'd just hoped that by some miracle she wouldn't be.

Whatever. Why focus on Marissa? There are new people to meet, a director and choreographer to impress. Time to join this theater company. I straighten my shoulders and step away from the door.

"Ellie!" A voice halts me.

I turn to find Gregor pointing happily at me. "I knew you'd get in. Congrats."

I point back at him. "You too."

He pulls me into a hug and rocks me back and forth like I'm his long-lost pal. It's great. Since the kids at my new school continue to be generally boring, Gregor's the closest thing I have to a friend now.

"Aha. You're just in time for the drama." Gregor swings me around to face the group. "The cast list is going up." He points to Neeta tacking a sheet of paper onto a bulletin board near the piano.

"Doesn't everybody already know their roles?"

"The ones who are double cast don't know who they're sharing a role with. Until now."

I'd half-forgotten Drew mentioned this when he called. Maybe I'd forgotten on purpose. Because now I feel a jitter of worry in my gut.

"I'm double cast," I tell Gregor. "I'm Piper."

Gregor steps back, looking dramatically shocked. "Your first show with YWTC and you're not in ensemble? You're a specific character? That's unheard of."

"Seriously? So this could be good?"

"Can't you tell by how jealous I sound? Go see who you're cast with." He points to the actors swarming the bulletin board.

But not everyone is swarming. I look sideways at Gregor. "It's only girls reading the list."

He looks caught out. "Fewer guys audition, so there are always roles for them. More girls audition, so..." He shrugs. "They have to share."

As if on cue, the guy Marissa was laughing with comes loping toward us. Gregor mutters, "Here comes surfer dude."

"Gregor, bro, heard you're playing Vincent. Major role. Sweet. I'm playing Dean. So stoked." He holds up his big hand for Gregor to high-five.

Gregor complies. "Cool, Brayden. We've got a couple of great numbers together." Gregor catches me backing away. "Have you met Ellie? This is her first gig with us. She's landed Piper."

"Who's Piper?" Brayden attempts to furrow his pale brows, but his face can't quite do it.

Gregor rolls his eyes. "A character in the play."

"I was just going to go check that out, Brayden. Nice to meet you." I abandon Gregor to his fellow we-get-roles-to-ourselves castmate.

I get to the back of the cluster of girls pointing at the list, all talking or whispering. I stand on tiptoe. Shantel glances over her shoulder and spots me. "Hey, you got Piper. Cool role."

"Thanks. I know."

I freeze. Because I wasn't the one who said that.

But I know the voice.

Right in front of me. Even the back of her head looks uptight somehow. Marissa. She said it. Marissa is Piper. I'm Piper.

Shantel laughs. "Yeah, you too, Marissa."

Slowly, following Shantel's eyes, Marissa turns around to face me. Her smile shuts down. "Seriously?" she says.

People buzz around us, focusing on their own news.

"Seriously," I say back.

*   *   *

Twenty minutes later, Neeta gives an ear-splitting whistle from the rehearsal table.

"Okay, people. You've all been given your scripts. Two minutes for any last bathroom breaks or super-important texts to your besties. Then it's butts in seats, phones off, brains on for our first read-through."

I'm standing off to the side of the room, still absorbing the shock of sharing Piper with Marissa. Nothing to do but heed Neeta's command. I sit in one of the chairs in the circle. I take a deep breath, look down at my copy of the script and smooth my hand over the cover. Neeta has penciled *Piper/Ellie* on the top right corner. I've always loved getting a new script. At Rossmere, Cassidy and I would huddle together counting our character's songs, scanning the pages for big chunks of monologue.

Someone sits beside me. I look up, ready to smile, and see Marissa. Is there no escape from her? I look away. Drew is walking around the room, talking to pairs of girls at a time.

"Actors who share roles are *supposed* to sit together," Marissa says in a tone implying I'm clueless. "It's how we always do the first read-through." She arranges her bag at her feet and puts her water bottle beside it.

"Fine. Nobody told me."

"That's what I'm doing now."

"Great."

She sits back in her chair.

I open the script and look for the song list. Out of the corner of my eye, I see Marissa roll her shoulders back and forth. "If you're looking for your solos, Piper has one. It opens the show. Lots of lines, but one solo."

"That's not what I was checking," I lie, swallowing my disappointment. One solo? I've never played such a small part. "I like to know what all the songs are before starting."

"You don't even know the play?"

"We just got the scripts."

"The *rehearsal* scripts." She gives a dismissive sniff. "Friendly advice? There are other ways to read a play before first rehearsal. Even better, watch a performance. I saw *Schooled* off-Broadway last summer."

Of course you did, Queen of the Theater. I lean down to get a pencil from my backpack and murmur under my breath, "I'm just going to throw up on you now."

"What?"

"Hey, Marissa, Ellie." It's Drew.

I bolt back up. "Hey, Drew!" Marissa and I say at the same time.

Drew laughs. "Very nice unison."

"It's like we're meant to play the same part." Marissa laughs and smiles at me like we're best buds.

Drew ignores her comment. "Ellie, could you do Piper for this read-through?"

"Sure." If I could high-five myself, I would.

He gives a distracted thumbs-up and moves on.

Delicious silence from Marissa.

"The order at the read-through doesn't mean anything, you know," she finally mumbles.

"Totally. But can we not talk right now? I like to focus before a rehearsal," I say, mimicking how she cut me off at the audition. I snap open my script to Act 2, Scene 1.

First read-throughs really are one of my favorite things.

Seven

Renée wraps up her welcome speech with, "It's time to open our scripts—and our hearts—and start our journey through the world of *Schooled*!"

Totally hokey but also totally exciting. We all applaud. Even Marissa.

"You heard the boss-lady," Neeta says. "Let's do this!"

She waits for us to settle, then reads out the first stage directions. "*Lights up. Headmistress Winterbottom's office at Moberly Prep School. The headmistress shakes hands with a new student, Hannah.*"

About six chairs over from me, a willowy girl called Claire flips her long blond hair over her shoulder. In a plummy voice, she says,

"Welcome to Moberly Prep, Hannah. I hope you are as proud to be here as we are to have you. Our first black student. The world is changing. Moberly must change too. You are helping us as much as we are helping you."

Across the circle from Claire, Shantel, playing Hannah, says, *"I can't wait to get started, ma'am."*

Drew paces behind the table, script in hand. I remember Mrs. Mowat at Rossmere sweeping across the stage when she gave us directions. Maybe all directors hate sitting still when they rehearse.

"Headmistress and Hannah freeze." Neeta's high voice projects easily. *"Tight spotlight on Hannah's head. She turns to audience."*

"Hang on," Drew says before Shantel can say her line. "The dorm set gets slid in behind Hannah here. Actors who are in the next scene, you'll be doing this set change. It's a quick one. One of our rehearsals will focus strictly on set changes. Okay, keep going, Shantel."

"How could I know what I was really starting? The first black student. Was Moberly Prep making a mistake? Was I?" Shantel already sounds in character.

Neeta continues, "*Hannah steps away from Headmistress Winterbottom, who silently exits.*"

Shantel goes on: "*I learned a lot at Moberly. Most of it wasn't about academics. But I sure got schooled.*"

"*Lights up on dorm room.*"

There's the sound of all of us turning our script pages together. I see Piper's song coming up. Cue crazy heart fluttering.

Neeta reads, "*One bed is tidily made up, the other appears to be piled with clothes and blankets. Hannah puts her suitcase down at the foot of the tidy bed. She steps toward the other bed.*"

I shift forward on my chair, hold my script out in front of me and swallow.

Neeta: "*Suddenly, blankets fly off. Piper jumps up and stands on her bed.*"

"*Welcome to your dorm!*" I declare.

"Nastier," Marissa says under her breath.

I whip my head to look at her, thrown off by the interruption. But she stares at her script, giving nothing away.

Drew interjects, "And we go into 'Welcome to Your Dorm' with Piper and the girls." He points at me, and I enjoy the feeling of everyone looking my way. Well, everyone except Marissa.

"We're not going to sing through the songs today," Drew says. "But I'll play a few bars to give a sense of the mood of each number."

He sits at the piano and bangs out a high-energy, rapid tune. I can't wait for the chance to sing it.

Drew talks over his playing. "Piper's leaping between the two beds, going around poor Hannah. In the second-to-last verse, one of you ensemble ladies will be coming in the window, one from under the bed, singing. A mini-swarm. Should be a fun, frenetic number. Camilla's got some great stuff worked out for the choreography. Good show opener. Okay, song ends, then Piper will say—"

"*Come on, shorty. You don't wanna be late for field hockey, do ya?*" Do I sound nasty now?

"Great," Drew says.

We move on to the next scene, one with Gregor's and Brayden's characters.

I sink back in my chair. So that's it for my big solo: two lines, one of which I apparently read wrong, and a song that'll give Camilla the chance to have me flinging around the stage.

I glance at Marissa's script in her lap. She's penciled all sorts of notes beside Piper's song. She notices me looking and makes a show of turning the page and leaning away from me. If Piper's supposed to be nasty, I'm thinking Marissa might be a natural.

* * *

During the break between reading the first and second acts, I go into the ladies' room, a drafty, two-cubicle thing. One of the cubicle doors opens and a girl about my age comes out. She's long-limbed and sunny-looking, with pixie-short hair. "Oh, hey. You're Piper, right?"

"One of them anyway. I'm Ellie." Bathroom small talk always feels weird to me, but the girl doesn't seem to mind.

"I'm Rachel," she says, looking at me in the mirror as she washes her hands. "This is my first play with Youth Works. Have you done a bunch?'

"No, I'm new too." I inch toward a cubicle.

"You're kidding." She yanks three paper towels out of the holder. "And you've got a big role like Piper?"

"I wouldn't call it big."

"A solo? That starts the show? I'd call that big. I'm in the ensemble. All of the fun, none of the pressure. I hope I get picked to be in your number. I'd love to be the girl coming in through the window. That's about as big a role as I'd want." Rachel crumples the towels into the hinge-topped garbage can beside the sink. "Nice to meet you, Ellie." She breezes out the door.

The garbage can's lid squeaks slowly to a stop. I watch it and think: I'm annoyed at sharing a good role with Marissa when I could be like Rachel, happy at the prospect of being in the ensemble and climbing through a window—if I'm lucky.

Neeta calls, "Two minutes, people."

Just enough time to adjust my attitude.

Eight

D rew spreads out the sheet music on the piano's rack. "This is a demanding number. You've got to punch it from the start and keep it jumping."

Good thing I did a voice warm-up at home this morning.

The rehearsal hall at ten o'clock on Sunday morning is quiet compared to Friday's first read-through. Marissa and I are the only ones at the piano with Drew, here for our first singing rehearsal. I was expecting Shantel too, but then I recall that though Hannah's in "Welcome to Your Dorm," she doesn't sing anything.

That's okay. I can hold my own against Marissa.

Drew rubs his hands together. It's the first week of fall, and we can feel it in the chilly room.

"I'll play the number for you once all the way through, and then we can work it verse by verse."

I get my script out of my backpack. I practiced the song at home a few times after Friday, so I'm feeling ready.

"Actually," Marissa says crisply, "I've got it memorized, so I'd love to dive right in, try the whole thing." She opens her script and smiles her big-teeth smile at Drew. "If that's okay."

"That's great. Diving in." He shifts the piano bench closer to the piano. "Pull up a chair if you want, Ellie."

I don't want. But I tuck the script under my arm, reach a chair off the stack under the nearest window and set it down beside the piano. I remind myself about Rachel's easy acceptance of being in the ensemble. I remind myself that I've always loved every part of rehearsals. I can make myself enjoy watching Marissa work.

She takes off her oversized knit scarf, circles her head a bit, stretches her mouth wide and shakes out her shoulders.

Yes, Marissa, we can see you preparing.

"Anytime," she says to Drew.

Drew rolls up the sleeves of his denim shirt. "Start with Piper's line, and then I'll come in."

Marissa plants her feet. Nods. "*Welcome to your dorm!*"

Doesn't sound any nastier than I did.

The intro is jangly and rapid, chipper yet bossy. Marissa sings, "*Welcome to your dorm / your home away from home / your palace on the quad. / That is if palaces are prisons / and homes are crowded pens. / The primitive conditions / might drive you 'round the bend. / Welcome to your dorm.*"

The rising notes on *drive you 'round the bend* are a bit out of Marissa's range. I shift forward on the chair.

She goes on: "*Welcome to your dorm / your shelter from the storm / the place to rest your head. / That is if 'rest' means squeaky bedsprings / a roommate who will snore / especially after sneaking / three beers and then four more—*"

Marissa mimes some wobbly drinking. Cute. But it doesn't hide that she's not landing those same notes.

"*Welcome to your dorm.*"

Drew stops playing. "Hold it there. The next bit is Piper with some of the ensemble. Those actors won't be here until..." He looks to Neeta, who's bustling in with an extra-large coffee.

"Eleven," she says. "You've got forty-five minutes."

Drew laughs. "How'd you know what I was asking?"

Neeta dumps an overstuffed messenger bag onto the table. "Mind reader. All stage managers are. Morning, chickies." She raises her coffee to Marissa and me. "Continue."

Drew turns back to us. "Remember, you're both ensemble for the performances when you're not Piper. So Ellie, join Marissa for this verse."

When I stand next to her, Marissa edges away. I shift closer just to bug her. She deliberately avoids eye contact.

"Piper stays on melody, ensemble on harmony. I'll sing it for you first, Ellie." Drew's telling me, not asking, like I'm probably not as prepared as Marissa.

He plays the music, singing the harmony, and looks at me to see if I've got it.

I nod.

Marissa and I sing, "*We know this isn't quite the place you were expecting / of academic sisterhood reflecting / the dreams of bright young minds busy connecting /with other bright young minds / together for this time / of brainy fun sublime—"*

Marissa snarks Piper's spoken line: "*Too bad.*"

Drew laughs and says, "Yes!" as he keeps playing.

Marissa carries on alone to the end of the song.

Neeta claps. "That number's awesome. Piper's such a weasel."

A weasel. I've never played a weasel before. I suspect Marissa has.

Drew rests his hands in his lap. "Terrific start, Marissa."

"Thanks. I love how wordy this song is. A fun workout for your mouth."

I'm tempted to point out that she ran some words together.

"Yeah, you really need to limber up before that one," Drew says. So I was right about her words running together!

Drew gestures to me. "Okay, Ellie, you ready?"

"Totally." I look at Marissa and wait for her to go sit in the chair this time.

She looks back at me. One thin eyebrow arcs the tiniest bit, just for me to see. "I should stay here for the ensemble part, right, Drew?"

"Perfect," he says.

Fine. Marissa can stand wherever she wants. This moment is what I'm here for. To be the fantastic singer I know I can be.

I launch easily into the first verse, belting the high notes. It feels great. A vocal bull's-eye.

Second verse, same thing.

When Marissa sings the ensemble part, I keep on belting. And when I end the song, Neeta puts down her bag of gummies to clap again. "Wowza. No surprise that you were cast."

Drew grins. "Good set of pipes."

I get a rush of warmth. I feel at home. I'm doing what I'm good at.

"Yeah, you've got a strong voice," Marissa says.

"Thanks. So do you." That's easy enough to say, knowing mine's stronger.

"But you know..." She tilts her head and pivots to face Drew. "Can I say something about singing as Piper?"

Oh-oh.

"Sure." He crosses his arms.

"Strength like that isn't right for Piper. She worries she's not good enough for the school. That's why she's mean to Hannah. I was showing her insecurity. Vocally." Marissa waves her slender hands between her throat and chest. In case we're not clear where vocals come from. "You can't just sing a song so it sounds good. You have to act it."

"And hit the notes," I can't help adding.

Drew gives a flicker of a smile.

Marissa laughs. "Obviously."

Even though she *obviously* didn't hit them.

"Good point, Marissa," Drew says. "That's the thing about musical theater. When characters can't express their feelings with words alone, they sing."

"And when singing's not enough, they dance!" Marissa exclaims, like she's hoping to win a game show. "Didn't Stephen Sondheim say that?"

"Honestly, I can't remember," Drew says. "But you're right about having to act a song."

Marissa looks down, doing her best to act modest about being right. Some acting job.

Drew flips the sheet music back to the beginning. "Let's do the Piper section again. How about both of you sing it together?"

"Great," I say.

But if I could sing and dance my real feelings about Marissa right about now, it'd be one noisy, foot-stomping number.

Nine

"Hold it!" Camilla shouts just as I'm about to leap off the wooden rehearsal bed. I freeze. Drew stops playing piano.

We're in the middle of choreographing "Welcome to Your Dorm." Rachel and Marissa, on either side of the bed, are my cheerfully malicious dorm mates in the number. We're giving Shantel's Hannah a rotten welcome.

Camilla looks up at me with her dark, kohl-lined eyes. "Ellie, don't broadcast your moves. If Hannah saw Piper's jump coming, she'd just get out of the way."

Shantel does an exaggerated moonwalk away. "I'm outta here, maniac."

I laugh and straighten from my half squat. "Got it. No cat-about-to-pounce-on-a-dust-bunny move."

"Exactly." Camilla smiles and gives my hand a quick squeeze before walking away. Drew was right—so far, working with Camilla is better than auditioning for her. She even knows my name now.

She leans against the table where Neeta takes notes. "Back to the top of the number, girls. Let's see if the pieces fit together."

"Great," I say.

I am feeling great. My jazz shoes don't kill me anymore. Camilla's worked us for over an hour, and I've kept up with the pace. I found a video online this week of another student production of *Schooled*. I had no idea if their choreography would be the same as Camilla's. But I needed some sort of preparation after Marissa's fully memorized singing at last rehearsal. It's paid off: a lot of the moves are similar to Camilla's.

Drew asks, "Everyone ready?"

"Yeah." I'm back to lying down under the itchy wool blanket, ready to surprise Hannah.

Marissa's "yes" comes from under the bed, where she's an evil dorm mate in cramped hiding. I know I'll have to do that part too, but I'm happy to let her rehearse it first. Though I have to hand it to Marissa—she hasn't made a peep of complaint or criticism today.

"Wait," Rachel says, sounding panicked.

I poke my head out.

She looks at the floor, where colored tape marks out the different entrances and exits. "I forgot already. Is this the window?"

Neeta leans across her table. "Nope. Blue tape's for the next song. This song's red. The window is stage left of you."

Rachel's face lights up, and she hops to her spot. "Thanks, Neeta." She smiles at me, and I give a thumbs-up and tuck my head back under the blanket. I'm happy to have Rachel at rehearsal. Her wish came true: she gets to be the girl who enters through the window.

"Let's go," Drew says. "Lights up. Hannah enters the dorm."

First, a brief silence in which I know Hannah is looking around, taking in her new home. I hear her step toward the bed. My cue is to be the sound of her suitcase hitting the floor. Shantel doesn't have that prop yet, so I listen for the *flump* of her dropped purse.

There.

I fling the blanket off and spring upright. "Welcome to your dorm." I spread my hands, sort of for effect, really for balance. It's hard to go from lying down to standing up in one smooth move. Or even one unsmooth move.

Drew plays the intro, and I jump off the bed and throw my arm up and around Shantel's strong shoulder. Feet planted wide, I sing the song's opening. I love the power of my voice filling my body and reaching out into every corner of the rehearsal hall.

I link my arm through Shantel's and march her around the room for the lines about palaces and prisons and primitive conditions. Then I spin her around. Shantel is great, already giving me lots of reaction to work with. She makes being mean feel awfully fun.

I half lounge on the bed for the squeaky bedsprings and snoring roommates bit. Drew's change to a minor key signals Marissa's entrance. She slithers out from under the bed as the two of us sing, "*We know this isn't quite the place you were expecting.*" I help her up, and we do an exaggerated waltz with Shantel wedged between us. Camilla assured us earlier that this will look good—and it'll be funny, since Shantel's about five inches taller than Marissa and I are.

Marissa's easy to waltz with. She even takes my lead. She's supposed to, but still, I'm surprised.

The three of us circle to the window, where Rachel is crouched. Marissa and I break apart. We mime opening curtains. Rachel pops up on "*with other bright young minds*" and pretends to climb through as she sings about "*brainy fun sublime.*" Her voice is sweet yet sly, and her harmony and Marissa's work nicely with my melody.

Shantel backs away until she half-falls onto the trunk at the foot of the bed. I leap onto the bed itself.

It's awesome to be so high above everyone else onstage. I can practically feel the warmth of a spotlight. I hold the high note at the end of the line "*we'll move in for the kill*" while Shantel cowers on the trunk. Then I jump down—smoothly this time—for another "*welcome to your dorm.*" Big nasty smile.

"It's working!" Camilla springs forward. "Nicely done for a first go-through. Ellie, you're a fast study." She sounds pleasantly surprised. Maybe even impressed.

"Thanks." I feel carbonated inside.

Marissa says nothing, her face a neutral mask.

Drew, still at the piano, asks, "Can we go through that section again, but with Marissa as Piper?"

Darn. I'm revved and ready to keep going.

"Let's do it." Marissa perks up and dusts off her leggings.

"A quick loo break first?" Camilla asks. She holds up an empty water bottle. "I've been hydrating too well."

"Omigod, I'm so glad you asked." Neeta pushes out of her chair. "Five minutes, ladies and gent." She and Camilla jog off toward the bathroom together.

Drew stands, stretches and scruffs his hand through his shaggy hair. "Guess I'll go grab some fresh air then. Good work, girls." He strides to the door, pulling on his slouchy sweater.

"Thanks," I call after him.

Shantel lies back on the bed, drapes her forearm over her eyes and quietly runs lines for her upcoming monologue. I'd like to tell her how fun she is to work with, but I don't want to interrupt her.

"Do you think there's any coffee left?" Rachel heads to the small table where Neeta has set up a metal coffee urn and a stack of cups.

"Coffee's bad for your voice. Every actor should know that." Marissa sits with her ever-present bottle of water. She and Camilla always drink like they're camels before a long trip.

"Good thing we're not real actors then," Rachel says.

"Speak for yourself," Marissa snaps.

"Totally am. Lighten up." Turning her back, Rachel hums as she pours her coffee.

I want to laugh but don't. Rehearsal's been great so far. Marissa's been in a good mood. I'd like to keep that going. I take my open script off the chair beside Marissa and sit down. "You're right about coffee."

"I know. That's why I said it."

Ah. There's the Marissa I know and don't love.

Rachel comes over with her coffee. "Call me a rebel then. I'm gonna risk it." She takes a sip. "Ugh, lukewarm. Oh well. Still drinkable."

Marissa busies herself with digging for something in the bag slung over the back of her chair.

As Rachel crosses in front of us, I notice Marissa's foot creep forward.

I stand. "Watch out—"

Rachel's foot catches on Marissa's. Her hands fly out to keep her balance. Coffee splashes over my script and part of my hand. I drop the script, and it lands in the fresh puddle of coffee.

"Omigod, Ellie, are you okay?" Rachel grabs my arm like she's afraid my hand is on fire.

"I'm fine. Lukewarm, remember?" I retrieve my dripping script. "This, not so much."

"I'll get some tissues." Rachel goes to Neeta's table.

Shantel glances over, then re-covers her eyes and keeps on with her monologue.

Marissa, casually sipping her water, regards me. "There goes your safety deposit on the script." Her foot is back under her chair. But her total lack of surprise makes me suspect Rachel's tripping was no accident.

"That's really all you have to say?"

"Oops?" Marissa deadpans. "Why would I have anything to say? I wasn't the one spilling stuff."

Rachel returns, and I crouch down to help her wipe up the coffee.

"Marissa, baby, you ready to be Piper?" Neeta calls. She's back from break, with Camilla close behind her.

"You know it," Marissa answers, bright-voiced. She caps her water bottle, saunters over to the taped stage area and hops onto the rehearsal bed. The bed I have to hide under now.

Ten

Gregor, Shantel and I grab three seats in a café near the rehearsal hall. The cozy place buzzes with people laughing, chatting, sharing stuff on their phones. Spoons clink against cups. The espresso machine hisses.

I texted Gregor after Friday's script soaking to see if he and Shantel could meet up before today's rehearsal. I'm hoping for advice on how to handle Marissa.

"We should put a *Schooled* poster up here." Shantel sets down her chai tea and muffin and shrugs out of her yellow puffer jacket.

I shift my chair closer to the low table. "The only place in my hometown this busy on a Sunday morning is the hockey arena."

Gregor grimaces. "Please never take me to your hometown."

I laugh. "Deal."

He lowers himself into the armchair, groaning. "My thighs are literally screaming from Friday's rehearsal. Camilla's trying to kill me."

"That's just called dancing, you big baby." Shantel whacks his leg.

"Ow!" Gregor rubs his thigh, pouting in my direction. "She's so heartless."

I settle in with my latté. I could watch Gregor and Shantel like a show.

Shantel, feet up on the table, points her cup toward me. "You don't hear Ellie whining. Camilla had her and Marissa jumping around like a couple of gymnasts before you and the other dudes showed up Friday."

"She did," I confirm.

"Easy enough for Marissa." Gregor blows on his coffee. "She was a wannabe gymnast before she converted to the wonderful world of musical theater."

"She was?"

Gregor nods. "She told me she was this total balance-beam babe till she was about twelve."

I can picture Marissa whipping through a routine. Finishing up with her arms and head flung back, laser-beam smile set to slay. Just her sort of thing. Too bad, for my sake, she's not still doing it. "Why'd she quit?"

Gregor shrugs. "Wearing those tight buns hurt her head? The scary-competitive gymnasts made her insecure? They'd make me insecure."

"Ha!" Shantel says. "Gregor insecure. As if." She checks her phone. "Rehearsal starts in fifteen. I can't wait to get going on 'Wearing the Colors.' That tune is outstanding."

"You and Claire are gonna shi-ine," Gregor says in a singsong voice.

"It's Ilona's turn at Headmistress today," Shantel corrects.

"Okay, Ilona's not as great as Claire, but you are still gonna shi-ine." Gregor clinks his cup with Shantel's.

"Like silver," she agrees, then takes a big swig of chai.

"Do you think some of that scary-gymnast attitude is still stuck to Marissa?" I lean back with my latté, try to sound casual.

"I guess she can be kind of intense," Shantel says. She turns to Gregor with a smile. "Remember in *Oliver*?"

"Oh yeah." Gregor laughs. "Toughest street urchin in the ensemble. Made Fagin looked like this total wimp. Marissa should have been Fagin. You know," he says to Shantel, "I'm still mad I didn't get to be the Artful Dodger."

She nods. "So right."

"Jonah was more like the Fartful Codger," Gregor grumbles.

"Burn!" Shantel laughs.

I plunk down my cup. "I'm just asking because I find Marissa kind of harsh. Like, she deliberately tripped Rachel at the rehearsal on Friday."

"What?" Shantel frowns. "I don't remember that."

Gregor stares into his cup like he's still brooding about the Artful Dodger.

"It was during the break," I tell Shantel. "You were busy practicing your monologue."

"Oh. When you spilled coffee on your script?"

"*She* spilled coffee on my script. I mean, Rachel spilled it, because Marissa tripped her." My temperature rises just remembering it.

Gregor looks up. "Marissa tripped you?"

Why aren't they getting this? I lean forward. "Not me. Rachel. After she told Marissa to lighten up. Marissa tripped Rachel so her coffee spilled all over my script. Marissa pretended it was an accident."

"That sounds complicated." Gregor scrunches up his nose. "Why would Marissa want to caffeinate your script?"

"Marissa was mad that Camilla said I was a quick study." I can hear myself getting louder.

Shantel raises her eyebrows.

"I'm not trying to brag. But Camilla complimented me, and that bugged Marissa."

"So she tripped Rachel," Shantel says, her voice flat.

"Marissa's intense. But she's never been nasty," Gregor says.

I have to raise my voice above the noise of the espresso machine. "Maybe she's never had competition before me."

There's a sudden small patch of silence. Shantel pulls back, her eyes narrowing. "I've been in the ensemble with Marissa for every show before this one. There've always been strong performers in the ensemble."

Gregor nods. "Marissa's solid."

"But she's never had to share a role before, right?"

"Have you?" Shantel shoots back.

"No. I've always had the lead." The minute I say it, I can feel it's a mistake.

"You know how I said you weren't whining earlier?" Shantel asks, dead calm. "Now you kind of are."

I go cold. It's as if the two of them are looking at me from the other side of a thick glass wall.

Then Gregor flings his hand up. "Oh, whatever. You and Marissa can hurl coffee at each other for all I care. As long as you're both awesome in the show, I'm good."

Shantel silently finishes her drink.

"I guess maybe Marissa tripped Rachel by accident," I say, though I still have my doubts. "Anyway, we should get going."

Shantel leads the way toward the door. Gregor moves in beside her and tucks his arm in hers. He starts singing, "We're Off to See the Wizard," and Shantel joins in. They skip through the café like an offbeat Dorothy and the Scarecrow.

I trail behind, not part of their little show. They've made it clear—if Marissa is a problem, she's all mine.

*   *   *

October drags along into November. The weather is gray, and school is dull. Cassidy calls too little and is too happy when she does. *Yes, I'm sure* West Side Story *was a smash, Cassidy.* Apparently, Mrs. Mowat says she can't imagine a better Maria.

Meanwhile, *Schooled* rehearsals have been for parts of the play Piper's not in. Marissa and I have more or less steered clear of each other while we've learned our bits in the big ensemble numbers "Missing Curfew," "Haze" and "Benefactor's Dance." On Friday—yesterday—I wasn't called at all. Drew was working the Hannah and Headmistress Winterbottom scenes. At least tomorrow we're doing a run-through of the whole play. Then rehearsals move into the theater next week.

"Admiring the view?" Dad's voice startles me out of my staring-blankly-at-the-window-from-the-couch coma. He plunks a delicious-smelling bag of food onto the kitchen island.

"I didn't hear you come home." I slap my science textbook shut and stretch my arms over my head.

He walks over to our huge window. "Looks kind of cozy, doesn't it? All those windows lighting up. Folks getting set for Saturday night in the big city."

I join him. "And you're having takeout Indian dinner with your daughter."

"Nowhere else I'd rather be." He puts his arm around me. The wind whines beyond the glass, spattering raindrops against it.

"Look." I point to the balcony across the way. "That dude barbecues in any weather."

"Barbecuing, musical theater...if you love something, you keep at it through thick and thin." Dad employs his chipper broadcast voice.

I elbow him away. "Gee, thanks for the public-service announcement." My stomach emits a rude gurgling noise.

"I get the hint." He goes to the kitchen. "Hey, I was chatting with Renée Felix today. Your artistic director?" he says, pulling takeout containers from the bag.

"Really? She call you for a date? You two looked pretty comfy together on your show that time." I set out dishes on the island.

"She did not call for a date." He blushes. "It was strictly professional. We were talking about her coming back on the show just before *Schooled* opens. Drum up some publicity." He gets a beer out of the fridge for himself and an iced tea for me. "She wants someone from the cast to do a song."

I'm wide awake now. This is way more interesting than Dad possibly getting a date. "Which song?" I know which one would be perfect. If I do it.

"She said she'd decide at the run-through tomorrow." He settles onto a stool and dishes out the food, like what he's just said is no biggie.

I'm scheduled to do Piper tomorrow.

I pull up a stool. "Did you tell Renée your talented daughter is playing Piper? And that her solo would be perfect because it sets up the whole play?" I try to sound like I'm joking around.

Dad stops his food serving and gives me a wry smile. "I thought my show was *awkward*. Now you're angling to get on it?"

"I meant some of the guests were awkward." I take a bite of naan bread. "And sometimes the host."

Dad throws a paper napkin at me. "Hoo-boy, for someone who wants me to pull some strings..." He shakes his head and cracks open his beer.

"I'm kidding. But did you mention me?"

"I didn't. I'm a professional, and she's a professional."

"What does that mean?"

He crosses his arms. "It means I'm not going to push my personal agenda on a guest. And she's not going to pick someone to represent her theater company based on a favor." He sighs. "Also, you wouldn't want to be picked just because I'm your dad, would you? You want to be picked because you're good."

I hate when Dad is right. I crack open my iced tea and don't answer.

He unfolds his arms. "Anyway, I still have to talk to my producer, Bev, to see if there's space in the schedule. So don't say anything to your castmates yet."

"Okay."

"Let Renée announce it when—if—it happens."

"Got it, Dad."

"Great. Cheers." He clinks his drink against mine.

I tuck into my dinner, but my brain is shuttering through images. Me singing "Welcome to

Your Dorm" on Dad's show. Renée and Drew telling me how fantastic I was. Marissa hearing them tell me that. The whole cast seeing me and loving it.

All I need to do is nail it at tomorrow's run-through.

Eleven

round the corner Sunday morning and spot
Renée dashing into the rehearsal building.
I pick up my pace, loving the almost tap-dance
sound of my boots on the cold pavement.

I'm so ready for today's run-through. I had
Dad wake me up early, before his morning run,
so I could do a super-complete voice warm-up.
I stretched every dance muscle I could. Riding
the subway, I relistened to Drew's recorded
accompaniment for "Welcome to Your Dorm" on
my phone.

I am set to knock Renée right out of her ankle
boots.

I burst through the rehearsal hall door and—
"Whoa!"—nearly crash into Rachel. She's bent

over, picking a muffin and a purple glove up off the floor.

She straightens, the other glove gripped in her teeth. "That was lucky," she says around it. Her free hand holds a large coffee.

"Lucky?" I scan the room for Renée. There. Standing at Neeta's table, talking with her, Drew and Camilla. Probably telling them about the possibility of showcasing *Schooled* on Dad's show.

"Yeah, lucky it wasn't coffee this time," Rachel says. "Remember your script? I could have soaked our artistic director. I didn't see her come in. Plowed right into her." Rachel hands me her gloves, including the one she's just taken from her mouth, so she can manage the coffee and muffin.

"You sure Marissa didn't trip you?"

Rachel laughs that off. "Positive. Randomly tripping is a special talent I've had all my life."

Before I can think that through, Rachel nods her head in Renée's direction. "Do you think she's staying for the run-through?"

"No idea." I can't reveal the real reason why Renée's here. "If she is, we just have to be great."

I go to hand Rachel back her gloves, and she points the pockets of her lime-green coat at me. I stuff the gloves in.

"Three-second rule," she says as she dusts off the muffin and takes a bite.

"Classy." The more time I spend with Rachel, the more I like her.

We go to join the other actors, but Neeta calls, "Ellie, can you come here for a sec?"

I go over. "What's up?"

Renée, Drew and Camilla have moved away from the table. Renée glances my way. I nod hello, but she's already gone back to her conversation.

Neeta finishes erasing something in her schedule. "Marissa has to miss the tech rehearsal when we move into the theater on Tuesday afternoon. She has a math test that day, and she can't skip it."

"Okay." I'm already looking forward to missing school for the tech and dress rehearsals this coming week, and now I can look forward to one of those rehearsals being Marissa-free.

"So I've asked her to do Piper for today's run-through. Then you can do Piper at the tech and take notes for her. A little swap-a-roo."

Little? With Renée scouting the rehearsal today? "I can do both. Today's and tech. I don't mind doing an extra one."

"You're a trooper. But it would be helpful for Marissa to get this run-through in before dress on Wednesday." Neeta reaches into her bag of gummy bears. The sticky-sweet smell gets up my nose. "She does Piper on opening night, remember."

Like I'd forget. "But if she gets all the tech notes from me and she's at dress, she'll be fine for—"

"Ellie, you just need to do what your stage manager asks you to do." Neeta's voice is blunt.

I back off. "Of course. No problem."

"Great." She pencils my name in her notes, then yells past me, "Five minutes to Act 1, people."

Retreating to my chair, I hear Drew say to Renée, "For sure. I'll leave that to you."

I stop. What if my swapping places with Marissa has nothing to do with her test? Maybe Drew is switching Pipers today because Renée's told him she needs to see the best performers.

Marissa sashays past me, humming "Welcome to Your Dorm" extra loudly.

* * *

I love the gleefully wicked look on Rachel's face when she and I crowd Shantel. We prowl like schoolgirl hyenas as we harmonize.

Even though I'm only doing my ensemble part, I'm determined to sing my heart out. I glance to where Renée sits, front row center. Her legs are neatly crossed in her trim black skirt, one foot keeping time with the music.

Her eyes focus on Marissa.

I make a quick calculation. When Piper's stand-on-the-bed moment happens, Rachel and I are supposed to be downstage, facing Hannah at the end of the bed. Instead, as we get to that point, I cheat my way upstage to the side of the bed. I hope Rachel will do the same, since we're supposed to mirror each other, but she sticks with the original choreography.

When Marissa hits the lines *"together for this time / of brainy fun sublime,"* I'm upstage from her and fully facing the audience instead of Shantel. I harmonize like I'm supposed to. But with more force on the high note. The note Marissa never quite lands. I hold it a second longer than her. I catch Renée turning her attention my way.

Marissa jumps off the bed and hits the ground with a slight wobble. Rachel reaches out to steady her, but Marissa bats her away. A Piper-like move, so it fits the moment. I think.

When the song ends, Renée applauds, then tops that with "Bravo!" She loves the number.

But whom did she love in it?

Twelve

When the run-through is done, we all anxiously wait for notes from Drew and Camilla. Renée is keeping them back, consulting at Neeta's table. I sit close by, pretending to look through my script. But soon Renée makes her exit with a wave and "See you all at the theater next week!"

I want to shout, *Have you picked a song for* This City This Morning*? And if it's "Welcome to Your Dorm," can I please be the one to sing it?*

Too many people around to safely do that. I close my script and stare at the cover. *Piper/Ellie.* I feel hyperalert yet drained. The run-through was harder than I thought it would be, especially knowing Renée was watching.

"Rehearsal notes, everyone," Neeta announces. "I want to see *pencils* out. *Write down* everything your fearless leaders tell you. So you *remember*." She jabs the air with her own pencil for emphasis.

Rachel and Shantel sit down on either side of me. "Bring it on," says Shantel. She pulls a sharpener out of her bag and hones her pencil to a lethal point.

Camilla stands in front of us, looking like a disappointed parent. Drew, beside her, runs his hands through his hair and surveys us with a weak smile. "So that was..." He lets out a long sigh.

"Rough," Camilla finishes.

"Come on," Rachel whispers beside me. "It wasn't that bad."

I nudge her to keep quiet.

"My overall note to everyone is"—Drew points to his ear—"listen. Listen both as your character and as a performer. Listen onstage, to every other person there with you, so that you are completely in the moment. Listen offstage, so you are always aware of the state of the show. Is your cue coming up? Is the energy flagging? Are you too loud backstage?"

Brayden drops his pencil, and Camilla darts a look at him.

"Musical theater is never about one character, one performer, one moment." Drew walks back and forth, propelled by what he says. "Each of you is part of the rehearsal or the performance for the entire time it is happening. Whether you're in the scene onstage or not." He comes to a dead stop. "If you are in the building, you are in the play."

I have a sudden need to cough. I swallow it away.

"If that level of attention is too difficult for you," Drew says, "then musical theater is too difficult for you."

"What he said," Shantel murmurs, and Gregor gives her a quiet low five.

Rachel and I exchange a wide-eyed look.

"Okay." Drew drops into a chair and smiles at us, like he's finished an unpleasant chore. "Let's get down to details."

Everyone seems to let out a breath.

"Claire and Shantel, tighten your reaction time in Scene 1. Brisk, Claire. Welcoming but brisk,"

Drew says. "Headmistress Winterbottom is working to keep her doubts in check."

Claire nods and makes a note in her script. So does Ilona, the other girl playing the headmistress. That makes me realize that even though I didn't get to be Piper today, I should take down any notes about her.

Drew continues. "Shantel, I liked the look you gave Headmistress when she froze. But make sure it's brief."

"Aww, no milking the moment?" Shantel tilts her head.

He laughs. "Absolutely no milking. Unless I say so. Then milk away."

A few kids laugh, and the mood in the room lightens. Phew.

"Now, 'Welcome to Your Dorm.'" Drew turns the page in his script and then looks for Marissa, Rachel and me. My throat tightens.

"Can I jump in?" Camilla asks. Drew agrees.

"Girls, it was fine, but *fine* is death for an opening number. The moves have to be sharp. Marissa, you need to land your jump off the bed clean. *Bam!*" She slaps her thigh for emphasis.

Marissa, a few chairs away from me, squirms until she gets Drew's attention.

He lifts his fingers off his lap in an *I've got this* gesture. "Ellie, you need to be careful about where you are at that point. Make sure you're facing Hannah, not the audience. You upstaged Marissa there."

Camilla nods.

"Upstaged?" Rachel blurts out.

Heat bolts up from my gut like lightning. *Please shut up, Rachel.*

"It's when one actor pulls focus from another by doing something upstage from that actor." Drew's expression is pained at even having to explain this. "You don't want to do that."

Marissa settles back in her chair. She's only half smiling, but I sense she's fully gloating.

I flutter my hand like a white flag of surrender. "Okay, sorry. Got it." I bend over my script and scribble *face Hannah* just to hide my burning face.

"Moving on," says Drew. "Brayden, your entrance was late."

I don't hear the rest. *Upstaged.* The word repeats in my head like a pulse. I flash back to my audition, when Gregor sneered, "Only amateurs upstage."

Rachel bumps my leg with hers and, as if she's read my mind, gestures to Gregor. He mouths *Ouch!* at me. Could be sympathetic, could be snarky. I haven't trusted him the way I did before he and Shantel shut me down about Marissa.

I look away and force myself to refocus on what Drew and Camilla are saying. Slowly, the sound of the other actors jotting notes settles me down enough to see that maybe I'm not the only one who messed up.

Although I am the only one who got a warning about upstaging.

How could I have been stupid enough to have thought this run-through was all about who should sing on *This City This Morning*?

Thirteen

Later, I come out of the bathroom to what looks like an abandoned rehearsal hall. The tall windows show the late-afternoon darkness outside. My tactic of stalling until everyone else leaves seems to have worked. But then I spot Drew and Neeta standing by the main door with Marissa. They don't notice me.

"We'll tell the rest of the cast on Tuesday." Drew's voice carries in the empty room. "Renée says it'll be great publicity. And being on a breakfast TV show will be fun for you."

So there it is. Marissa's going to do the appearance on Dad's show. I'm not surprised, after how I performed—or didn't—today. I'm not even that disappointed. I just want to go home. But I have to get past them. I don't want to face Marissa after being busted for upstaging her.

I duck my head and dig for my phone in my backpack as I speed toward the door.

"Hey, Ellie," Marissa calls. "Thanks for agreeing to do the tech rehearsal for me."

She has that sheen of happiness people get when they're holding back exciting news.

"No worries. Good luck with your test."

"Rest up. Hydrate. Tech and dress rehearsals are intense." Neeta wags a warning finger at me.

"It's always great to get into the theater." At least Drew sounds a positive note. "You'll see, it makes a huge difference."

Meaning maybe I'll up my game there. "I can't wait," I say and hustle out of the building so they can get on with planning Marissa's breakfast TV debut without me.

Out in the cold, I turn my phone back on. Instantly, a text pops up from Cassidy. **You haven't liked my post yet. All the cast party photos!!!**

I haven't liked it because I haven't looked at it. I'm afraid that I'll miss everyone in the shots too much. Or maybe that I won't. Rossmere seems so long ago.

I keep walking and text, **Have tech & dress, then opening Thurs. So busy. So behind on homework. :(Will check out post soon.**

I've barely hit *Send* when my phone rings.

"Hey, Dad," I answer, ducking into a coffee shop to get out of the cold.

"Hey, El. Good rehearsal?" He sounds rushed.

"Yeah, fine." I'm not about to cough up all the grim details. "I'm nearly at the subway, so I'll be home in fifteen."

"I won't be. That's why I'm calling. Work thing."

"It's Sunday night."

"I know. Sorry. There's leftover butter chicken in the fridge."

I get in line behind the other customers. I'd rather grab some "artisanal" sandwich and sit with a bunch of strangers than go eat leftovers in an empty condo. "Great."

"Also, I talked to my producer about someone from *Schooled* coming on to the show." He clears his throat. "The good news is Bev says we've got space on Wednesday morning...so..."

So that leaves the bad news. He knows. Renée probably called him right after she left the rehearsal hall. I have zero desire for sympathetic parent blabber. "I know, Dad. The bad news is it's going to be Marissa, not me. It's fine. Renée made her choice."

The woman ahead of me orders three of the most convoluted drinks possible.

Dad goes on: "The thing is, El, I was the one who told Renée she should pick a song you're not in."

The woman says, "And make sure the grande is skinny."

"What?" I leave the lineup and go stand by the window. "But last night you said she didn't even know I was your daughter."

"That was before I talked to Bev this morning. She gave the spot a green light, as long as we avoid anything that looks like conflict of interest. It's station policy. Renée needed to know that before she picked someone."

"Wait—before? When did you tell Renée?" A guy opens the door, letting in a gust of cold air.

"After I talked to Bev." There's a pause. "This morning. Before your rehearsal."

"I thought you went for a run," I say. Stupidly. Like it matters.

"I'm sorry if you're disappointed. It's still great publicity for the play. You'll get bigger audiences. Renée is very excited."

"I bet." It suddenly seems weird for Dad to be so comfortable talking about Renée. "Um, I'm heading into the subway now, so I'm going to lose the phone signal. Have a good work thing."

I get back in line, order my sandwich and hot chocolate, and take them to the high counter against the window. I watch people and traffic go past as I eat. And think.

Renée knew coming into today's run-through that I couldn't do the *TCTM* spot. So her picking Marissa had nothing to do with Drew changing who played Piper today. It also had nothing to do with my upstaging Marissa. Renée probably didn't even spot that—she wouldn't know Camilla's choreography.

It's a small comfort. I still messed up. And Marissa's still going to get all the attention.

My phone buzzes with another text from Cassidy. **Send photos of your big-city theater for me! I'm suffering show withdrawal :(**

It's as if she's finally remembered I'm doing a show too. I text that I will, then go to my phone's photos. There's the shot I took of the rehearsal hall on the day of the first read-through. I stare at it and try to put myself back into the music, the sunlight, the anticipation of that day. But it's as if everything that's happened since then has upstaged all that excitement.

I finish my food and join the stream of people hurrying through the chilly November night.

Fourteen

"Close your eyes. You need to do your first entrance right." Gregor links his arm in mine as we stand outside the Sidestreet Theater. The word *Backstage* is stenciled in yellow letters on the beat-up metal door in front of us.

"Is this some weird theater tradition I've never heard of, where newbies are brought in like hostages?" I can see my breath. Despite the midday sunshine, the air is frosty, and I just want to get inside.

"Wow, harsh. You need to have a little more trust in your fellow actors." Gregor purses his lips.

I laugh. "Okay. Don't be so dramatic."

"Dramatic is my default mode, girlfriend." He wriggles his fingers at my eyes, hypnotist-style. "Now, close them."

I do as I'm told. That's my game plan after messing up at Sunday's run-through. *Stick to the script, Ellie.*

The door squeaks open. "One short step up," Gregor says.

I let myself be led up and then a few steps forward. The sounds of wind and cars die down, and then the door cranks shut with a bang. I flinch.

"You're fine, you big chicken." Gregor's voice travels only a few inches in the deadened air. And even though I can't see, I sense the dimness here compared to the brightness outside.

"Now, breathe it in," he says.

A musty but dry smell. With an undercurrent of hairspray and makeup. Also paint. "It's not pretty," I say. "But I like it. Can I open my eyes?"

"You may," Gregor declares, a wizard granting permission.

We're in a narrow passageway. The black walls are chipped, probably from earlier show crews knocking awkward props against them.

Gregor still holds my arm. "That was a test. Only true performers understand the beauty of this smell." He wafts the air toward his nose with one hand. "Glorious eau de backstage."

"So I passed? I'm a true performer?" I try not to sound desperate.

"I didn't say this was the only test. We still have to see how you get through tech and dress and opening and second night and—"

"I get it!" I whack his arm the way Shantel would. "Can you just show me where to go now, oh True Performer?"

"That's the spirit." He takes me toward the stage and the voices of our castmates.

The day stretches ahead of me, full of the pleasure of being Piper. And no Marissa to spoil it.

* * *

Tech rehearsals were never this detailed in the poky Rossmere auditorium. Rachel and I have shifted the two dorm-room beds and the window wall onstage and off three times. I've had to make quick notes about every entrance and exit and set shift in my script to pass on to Marissa.

Now Rachel, Shantel and I stand squinting out to where Drew and Neeta sit in the middle of the darkened audience section—the house. They're in a circle of light cast by the desk lamp clamped to their makeshift table. They look awesome out there, like the classic movie image of a director and stage manager.

Drew was right about things feeling different once we got into the theater. It's miles better than the rehearsal hall. The show is starting to form into a real thing.

"We should do that one more time, girls," Drew says. "So you're solid with getting everything in place."

"And so Cheng can lock in the timing for the cross-fade after Shantel's spotlight," Neeta adds.

Cheng, the twentysomething sound and lighting guy, pokes his spiky-haired head out of the control-booth window at the back of the theater. "Don't worry, people—you've only got about four and a half more hours of this torture."

"We love you, Cheng," Neeta shouts sarcastically over her shoulder.

He gives a cheesy grin and a thumbs-up and goes back to his adjustments.

Neeta says something into her headset's small mic.

In the wing beside me, Lucy, Neeta's red-headed friend who is working as our stage-crew person, replies into her own headset, "Got it." She calls out, "Headmistress Winterbottom, back onstage with Hannah, please. Piper and roommate, back in the wings."

Ilona—"the lesser Headmistress," as Gregor has privately nicknamed her—emerges from backstage to join Shantel. I go to the foot of my bed in the stage-left wing; Rachel goes to hers, stage right. When we hear our cue, we have to get the beds in position and lock their wheels in place. Then Rachel has to bring the window wall out and crouch behind it until her line in the song. All of this in dim lighting behind Shantel in her spot.

For now, though, we all stand at the ready.

Cheng calls, "All set here."

Drew says, "Shantel, take it from *I can't wait to get started.*"

And we start the scene again.

*   *   *

"So, Marissa's gonna be a celeb." Brayden, hands in the pockets of his artfully ripped jeans, walks backward to face the rest of us. He, Gregor, Shantel, Rachel, Ilona and I are on our way to grab a quick bite. Renée showed up just before our break to announce Marissa's appearance on *This City This Morning*. Too bad Marissa couldn't be here to act humble while soaking up the glory in front of us all.

"I don't know if being on some local morning show makes anyone a celebrity," Ilona sneers. She's the more judgmental of the two Headmistress Winterbottoms. "Who even watches those things anymore?"

I'd like to elbow her in defense of Dad. I can make fun of his show, but no one else should.

"Oh, my mom watches, that's who." Shantel projects like she's still onstage. Passersby turn to look. "Every morning before she goes to work, I hear her crushing on the host dude: *That Mark is one fine cut of prime beef!*"

I practically choke. But I can't help correcting her. "It's Mike."

"Oh-ho, you're a fan too?" Gregor says, shaking his hand like he's burned it. "Older man!"

"He's my dad."

That gets their attention. They all stop dead. Two guys shoot us dirty looks as they have to detour around us.

"Get. Out." Gregor faces me.

"It's true," I say. "Mike Fisk, *This City This Morning* host. Ellie Fisk, daughter of." I start walking again so we don't keep blocking the sidewalk.

"Cool." Rachel gives her laid-back approval. "I bet it was your idea for them to do a spot about *Schooled*."

"Uh, well—"

Before I can clarify, Brayden says, "I bet being him would be an awesome job."

"He does a pretty good job of being him already," I say.

The others laugh, and Brayden goes, "Right... right. Still, I think I might have to look into that idea." He gazes off into the distance.

If I'd known I'd get such a great response to my dad being the *TCTM* guy, I might have confessed to it sooner.

We step into a pizza place. As we line up for slices, Shantel asks, "Why aren't you going on the show? Since he's your dad."

"'Cause it'd be weird?" Ilona says.

"Actually, Renée was thinking of me doing the appearance."

The words come out of me so easily it's almost scary. Although, strictly speaking, there's no proof Renée *wasn't* considering me before she knew I was Mike Fisk's daughter. I hurry on with, "But Dad said the station policy wouldn't allow it."

"That sucks," Brayden sympathizes.

"Anyway," I say, "I thought she should have chosen you, Shantel. You are the lead."

I should stop surprising myself with what I'm saying. None of this seems to fit my morning stick-to-the-script plan.

"Uh-uh." Shantel shakes her head. "If I went on your dad's show, my mom would explode. Literally." She pauses, looking thoughtful. "Marissa will represent. That girl works herself so hard, she deserves a little glory."

No doubt Marissa would agree. This time I have no problem keeping my mouth shut.

Fifteen

I hear Dad leave for work at four in the morning. Same as always. I burrow farther under my duvet.

My brain snaps on. Marissa's singing on his show this morning.

When I came home from tech rehearsal close to nine last night, Dad was already in bed. But he'd left a sticky note for me on my bedside lamp: *Hope tech was good.* Schooled *spot airing 7:45 tomorrow if you want to watch. (It's ok if you don't.) Love you!*

I don't want to watch. Or maybe I do. But what if she's great?

I turn over and force myself to go back to sleep. At least I have the pleasure of missing another day of school.

* * *

Before the dress rehearsal, girls take turns checking themselves out in front of the one full-length mirror in our crowded and cluttered dressing room. Putting on our Moberly Prep uniforms makes the world of the play feel suddenly real. Also, it's an excellent distraction from waiting for Marissa to swan in from her *TCTM* appearance. Which I did not watch. But which some people have said was *so great!*

Pulling the itchy wool skirt on over my dance shorts, I say to Claire, "You have to wear this stuff every day?" She goes to a private school.

Claire is buttoning up her headmistress blouse. "Have I mentioned how happy I am to graduate in six months? University sweatpants, here I come."

Shantel takes command of the mirror. "I think I rock this look." She flips up the lapels on her blazer. "Look out, Moberly, 'cause Hannah's comin' to shake you up."

There's a knock at the door and Lucy pokes her head in. "Neeta wants me to remind everyone that I have authority to kill you if your phones are on during rehearsal."

Her voice is much softer and sweeter than Neeta's, so it's almost funny to hear her threaten us. But when she gives a pointed look to Ilona and a few ensemble girls caught in mid-text, they quickly power off their phones.

"Thank you," Lucy says. "And Drew wants everyone onstage for vocal warm-up."

"Right now?" I ask, adjusting my necktie.

"Right now."

"Marissa's not here yet," Shantel points out.

And she's supposed to be doing Piper for this rehearsal.

Rachel, sitting with her feet up on the makeup counter, raises her eyebrows at me. She told me earlier that she didn't watch Marissa this morning either: *Well, I slept in. But even if I was awake, I probably wouldn't have watched.*

Lucy puts her headset back on. "Renée called. She took Marissa out for breakfast after the show. They're five minutes away." She leaves.

"Ah, celebrities," Rachel says, dropping her feet to the floor and standing. "Keeping us nobodies waiting."

"Come on." I link arms with her. "Time to warm up. No rest for the nobodies."

* * *

Marissa's timing is off all the way through Act 1. Then, as soon as lights come down on "Hazing Hannah," the Act 1 closing song, she breaks away from the rest of us and beelines backstage.

Drew's voice cuts through the dark. "Remember what I said at tech: hold position for a five-count before exiting."

"I gave Marissa that note last night," I whisper to Rachel, who's beside me in the end-of-song tableau.

I gave Marissa all the Piper notes when she showed up near the end of the tech rehearsal. There were a lot. Which I'd written out for her. Then she left before everyone else because she had to get up *so early, you know.*

"It's not your problem," Rachel whispers back.

The stage and house lights come up. Neeta, beside Drew in the back row, says, "Very short break, for necessities only. Bathroom, costume fixes, makeup refresh. Do not leave the building.

Be in your places for the top of Act 2 in fifteen minutes. Lucy will call you."

As Gregor and Shantel walk past me, I hear him ask, "Think something's wrong with Marissa?"

"Only all the time," Rachel jokes to me.

"Nah," Shantel answers Gregor. "Dress rehearsals are always wonky."

But as we all head backstage, I feel an uneasy twinge in my gut.

*   *   *

Most cast members are already back in the wings when Lucy calls into the backstage hallway, "Two minutes to places, please."

Marissa finally comes out of the ladies' bathroom.

"Are you okay?" I'm standing right outside the door, feeling a little like an ambushing fan.

A feeling made stronger by the startled and then annoyed face Marissa makes. "Of course I'm okay. I was just so rushed this morning I hardly had time to pee." She hurries past me, leaving a faintly sweaty smell in her wake.

"Right. Great job on *This City This Morning*, by the way," I say after her. It's like my guilt for staking out the bathroom, or for not watching her this morning, or for...something, is making stupid things come out of my mouth.

Marissa stops and turns back to face me in the narrow passageway. She looks pale. "I know you didn't watch the show. Ilona said you were practically bragging about that fact to Rachel. Way to support the play, Ellie."

I feel the color drain from my own face. "I wasn't bragging. I mean—"

"It must be embarrassing that your own dad couldn't convince Renée that you'd be a good choice to do a song on his own show."

"That's not how it works," I say.

She keeps on, pinning me to the spot with words. "Even though I'm sure you were desperate for the chance. The whole time we've been rehearsing, you've been desperate for people to notice how good you are. You had to resort to upstaging me so people would notice you. You think you're good just because you get the same role as me. On your first audition.

Without having been part of this company for three years. Like I have. Without putting in your time in the ensemble." She takes a shuddering breath in and out. "You're good, but you're no better than anyone else in this company. At least Renée and Drew and Camilla know that. That's why they wanted me to do the song this morning, not you."

Other cast members not needed at the start of Act 2, have come out of the dressing rooms while Marissa's been saying all this. They keep a safe distance back, even Gregor, like witnesses to a robbery. I'm in a spotlight of humiliation.

Marissa gulps in another breath. "And you know what?" She blinks.

"What?" The word barely makes it past the wedge in my throat.

There's a painful pause while her mouth moves as if working out the most devastating thing to say to me. Her eyes widen.

I step forward. "Marissa?"

She throws up at my feet.

Sixteen

look at Marissa's hair hanging down as she's bent over, and I feel everything turn to slow motion.

An ensemble girl going, "Whoa!"

Someone else saying, "I'll get Lucy."

Footsteps running away.

"Marissa?" I repeat. I should help her, but I feel trapped by what's between us. Literally. "Are you okay?"

Still looking down, she leans one hand against the wall and presses the back of her other hand against her mouth. From behind her hand she says, "Obviously not." She lifts her face and gives me a look that's equal parts contempt and sadness. "Guess you get Piper to yourself now."

Time speeds back up. Lucy squeezes past two ensemble guys hovering behind Marissa.

She takes in the view and pulls her headset mic to her mouth. "Neeta? We have a problem."

*   *   *

The lights come up again at the end of Act 2. None of us onstage move. Out in the third row, Drew is leaning forward, forearms resting on the seat in front of him. Camilla stands in the aisle beside him, hands in a praying position under her chin.

"Well," Drew says, pivoting in his seat to face Camilla. "That went surprisingly well."

"Nothing like a little trauma to focus a cast," Camilla answers.

They come to the stage, clapping, and everyone around me whoops and claps with relief. I make the effort to act happy too. I am glad we did a good job. But I worry that everyone's looking at me differently.

The scene with Marissa outside the bathroom plays on a sickening loop inside my head. Sickening not because of what she did but because of the truth she told.

I was desperate. For a role. For attention. For center stage. And that was more obvious than any talent I may have thought I had.

Camilla hugs one of the younger girls. She took over the ensemble part Marissa and I do when we're not Piper. "You were stellar, Darci! You fit right in to the choreography, and you got those couple of lines. Very professional. Did you happen to memorize Act 1 as well?"

"Totally," Darci says, beaming up at Camilla like a bloom facing the sun. "I just paid attention at every rehearsal."

Camilla turns to Drew. "Problem solved. If Marissa's still sick tomorrow—"

"Has anyone checked in with her?" I burst out. "Since her mom came to get her?"

That turns down the volume on the general congratulations-all-around party.

"Good point, Ellie. We shouldn't get ahead of ourselves," Drew says. He puts a hand on my shoulder. "Neeta said she'd call Marissa's mom as soon as we're done here. By the way, you did a great job stepping in as Piper with no notice. Especially after..." He pauses, pushing his glasses up his nose.

After the barf? After being revealed as a desperate attention hog?

"Thanks" is all I say.

Gregor gives a "Brava!" from across the stage, and Rachel, Shantel and a few other people clap.

But I'm relieved when Drew deflects the attention with "Okay, all, let's go sit. Camilla and I have a few final notes before tomorrow. Opening night, people!"

* * *

A little while later, Gregor and I wait together outside the theater for Shantel and Rachel so we can all walk to the subway. It's a cool, clear night with no wind, and the fresh air feels good after the stuffy dressing room.

"So it's good Marissa had food poisoning," Gregor says.

"Are you kidding?"

"I mean, good it wasn't some nasty bug that would have wiped her right out of the show. Bad, of course, that her fancy restaurant breakfast sausages were past their best-before date."

We had gotten these gritty details from Neeta at the end of notes from Drew. Including the fact that Renée had only had cottage cheese and fruit for her breakfast and so was fine. And that Marissa "guaranteed" Neeta she'd also be fine and ready to play Piper on opening night.

"It must have been the bad sausage talking when Marissa said those things to you today," Gregor says. "I'm sure she'll apologize when she sees you."

I'm not so sure. Do people apologize for being right?

We're quiet for a bit. We watch an orange cat trot across the empty street to scout out a garbage bin behind a building.

"Gregor, why did you decide to help me at my audition?" I ask without looking at him.

He shifts from foot to foot, keeping warm. "Because you looked like Snow White, remember?" He gives a little laugh.

"That's not a real reason." I shove my hands deep in my jacket pockets.

"Really?" He sighs. "Because you looked so lonely." His voice is simple, not a hint of funny, dramatic flourish to it.

I flash back to September, me sitting on that hard bench with my one song, Marissa and her binder of songs throwing serious shade my way. I didn't know a soul in this city. Loneliness must have been wafting off me in waves. Then I met Gregor. My eyes start to sting with tears.

Gregor, as if he senses that, tucks his hand in the crook of my arm. The same way he did when he first led me into the theater.

"It hit me right here," he says as he flattens his hand over his heart. "And I thought to myself"— now he swings out to face me, taking my hands in his in a cliché musical-theater move—"Gregor, this girl needs you!"

I have to laugh. He laughs too and lets go of my hands. I quickly wipe at my tears.

"Thank goodness you could actually sing." He bumps up against me, arm to arm. "I don't know what I would have done if you were crappy. Kicked you to the curb, I guess. *Scram, sister!*"

The orange cat scurries down the block. We laugh again.

Voices come from behind the backstage door.

"Finally," says Gregor. "Was someone offering free manicures in there or something?"

One more thought hits me. "Wait. So I'm here because of your pity?"

"Omigod, now who's being the dramatic one? Nobody gets cast in musical theater because of pity." He looks me straight in the eye. "Seriously. You're talented, Ellie. You belong here."

Shantel, Rachel, Brayden and Claire pile out of the theater, and we start off for the subway. Gregor shouts, "Well, my lovelies, shall we sing?"

"No!" we all answer.

The moment makes me think of Drew explaining the basis of musical theater. How characters need to sing when talking isn't enough, how they need to dance when singing isn't enough. I could sing and dance how wonderful it feels to be with Gregor and everyone right now. But in real life, after everything Marissa said to me, just being with them is enough.

Seventeen

I wake up before my alarm has a chance to go off. Tonight's opening night.

After a restless night replaying yesterday in my head, I know there's one thing I need to do before I can get on with today. I reach beside my bed, haul my laptop off the floor and plop it onto my duvet. I pull up the TCTM site. There's Dad, smiling like Mr. Good Morning in front of the city skyline. The thumbnails of videos from past shows line up below him. I click on the one titled "YWTC gets *Schooled*."

There's an intro bit between Dad and Renée. Dad tells a lame theater joke. Renée laughs. He beams at her. She touches his arm. They're even cuter with each other than they were during her first appearance back in September.

I'm going to have to think about what all *that* might mean some other time.

I scroll the bar at the bottom of the video until I see Marissa come into view. I let it play.

She's alone in a column of light. The Moberly Prep uniform makes her look younger. When Marissa or I perform "Welcome to Your Dorm" onstage, we are with castmates and in almost constant motion. And when we're in the ensemble, we never actually have a chance to watch closely how the other one performs. Now, alone on the bland TCTM set, Marissa simply stands there and sings.

Even though she's still, I can hear the whole action of the song in her voice. Yes, she hits the notes strong, gets the timing dead-on, sings each word clearly. That's impressive enough. But she makes Piper come to life.

I remember the first vocal rehearsal we had with Drew. I thought Marissa was making excuses for her singing when she said Piper felt insecure and that's why she was mean to Hannah. Now she shows me the truth of that. Marissa understands Piper's insecurity. And she makes the audience understand that too. The fear behind the swagger.

When the song's over, Dad, Renée and the off-camera tech people clap as the camera holds on Marissa's face. She looks straight into it. I feel like she's looking at me, asking, "Do you get it now?"

I do.

I close the laptop. I'm glad Marissa's going on as Piper tonight. She deserves it.

*   *   *

I'm just about to go into the theater when my cell phone buzzes.

"Hey, Dad." I pause at the backstage door. "How's the day?"

"All good. How was school?"

"Made way better by the fact that I knew I had a show to open tonight."

He laughs. "I just called to say 'break a leg.' I'm looking forward to tonight."

Claire and Ilona come around the corner and head toward the theater.

"It's Marissa's night to be Piper," I remind Dad.

"I'm coming to every performance," he reminds me.

I hadn't even thought about how nice it will be to know Dad's out there in the audience again. Like back in Rossmere. "Aww, you've always been my biggest fan," I joke.

"And I always will be," he answers. No joke.

"Back at you."

Claire mouths *Hi* and Ilona ignores me as I step out of the way so they can get inside.

"By the way," Dad says. "Renée tells me there was a spike in ticket sales at the box office after, uh, she was on the show yesterday."

It's cute how he avoids mentioning Marissa. "Awesome. Also by the way, I had a chance to watch the spot online this morning."

"Oh yeah?" He sounds like he's bracing himself for my opinion.

"Marissa was great. You're going to like watching her tonight."

"She was, kiddo. It's nice you can see that. Of course, I only watch you if you're onstage."

"Now you're being ridiculous." But I love him for saying that. I pull open the backstage door. "I better go. See you later, fanboy."

*　*　*

The cast has nearly finished the onstage vocal warm-up when Marissa walks through the audience entrance.

"Nice of her highness to grace us with her presence," whispers Rachel.

I watch Marissa sidle past the last-row seats to get to Neeta, sitting right beneath the control booth.

"One last roll down from standing, everyone." Drew stands facing us, not noticing. He's decked out in his version of opening-night formal wear: non-faded jeans, new high-top sneakers, a blazer and a yellow-and-green-plaid tie. "Hang from your hips like a rag doll. Let your spine, your shoulders, your neck, everything relax. Release any tension."

My tension decides to stay put. Something about being bent over like this reminds me of Marissa bent over outside the bathroom yesterday, steadying herself with one arm. Why isn't she hurrying to join us onstage?

"And slowly roll back up," Drew continues.

I do. Marissa is now sitting down. Neeta is standing beside her, hands on hips, staring holes into Drew's back. But she lets him finish.

"We're forty-five minutes away from lights-up. Fifteen minutes from the house opening." We can already hear our soon-to-be audience chatting and laughing as they wait to be let in. "You guys have worked so hard all these weeks. Now all you need to do is—" he puts his hand up to his ear.

"Listen!" we all shout.

He grins through his beard. "Music to my ears. Have an amazing show, everyone."

I hang back as my fellow performers stream offstage to the dressing rooms. Drew turns, sees Marissa, hops off the stage.

"Bring Ellie," Neeta tells him.

Marissa's eyes meet mine. There's the same sadness I saw yesterday. But none of the contempt.

* * *

"I'm sure you'll be fine, Marissa," I say. "It's probably just nerves. I know my heart's fluttering like a—"

"It's not nerves." She shakes her head like a stubborn kid. "I missed tech because of some stupid test. I missed half a dress rehearsal and could barely pay attention for the half I was there. I'm not ready. I'll let everyone down."

"We know you'd never do that," Neeta says.

Marissa looks up at Neeta. "My stomach still feels kind of odd."

Neeta and Drew exchange *uh-oh* looks.

Then they and Marissa turn to me.

The house manager cracks open the door and calls, "Can I please let the audience in? It's getting crowded out here." Voices carry from behind her like a cheerful mob.

"But it's opening night, Marissa," I say. That has to trump everything, doesn't it?

Two days ago, I never would have believed I'd be arguing with Marissa that she, not me, should perform Piper. But after what she said to me yesterday, and after watching her sing this morning, and realizing how it must have felt to put in three years with YWTC before getting a good role..."I'm happy to just be in the ensemble for tonight," I say.

Marissa's eyes narrow. "You should never say *just* be in the ensemble."

My breath catches. "You're right. I'm honored to be in the ensemble."

Then she smiles at me as if, for the first time, we're equals.

"Well, this is all very heartwarming, but you girls do know this is a decision for the director to make, do you not?" Neeta bursts out, her hand flapping at Drew as if he's missed an important cue. "At least get out of here so I can open the house? Then feel free to let me know who's doing what tonight." She puts on her headset and stomps away. "Twenty-five minutes to curtain, by the way." She flings the words over her shoulder.

Marissa laughs as she, Drew and I hustle out of our seats. "Neeta's my hero," she says.

"We need to give your hero an answer," Drew says.

Marissa looks at me, and I know what she wants me to say.

So I do. "You should be Piper tonight."

Another thing I've learned doing this play. An actor can only make a line sound true if she really feels it.

Eighteen

Marissa belts out the opening to "Welcome to Your Dorm." I can feel her voice coming right through the bottom of the bed. I see Shantel's kneesocked and sensible-shoed feet lit by the warm stage lights. The energy of a sold-out theater sizzles through me like a current.

It all adds up to the best feeling I know. And I'm still lying, unseen, under a bed.

When Marissa sings, "*But only after sneaking / three beers and then four more,*" I brace myself. Ready. Set.

"*We know,*" I sing as I slide out from under the bed and take Marissa's hands, "*this isn't quite the place you were expecting.*"

For the next two hours, we propel ourselves through the world of the musical. Where we both belong.

* * *

After the bows, after the applause, after the back-stage hugs and high fives and cheers and more hugs, I collapse into a dressing-room chair to catch my breath. Rachel's on the chair beside me, texting someone on her cell. "Neeta said it's okay once the show's over," she says when she notices Ilona watching her. She fist-bumps me. "Long live Neeta."

Brayden sticks his head partway through the change-room door. Two of the younger girls scream. He laughs and says, "Not looking. Letting y'all know opening-night party's at my place, whoever's up for it. No drinking. Much singing. Neeta's got directions if you need them. Thank you for your attention. YWTC rocks!" He closes the door.

"You going?" Shantel asks, catching my eye in the mirror as she wipes off her makeup.

"You know you were totally amazing tonight," I say. "You held that stage solid for two hours."

She tosses the tissue into a garbage can and turns to face me. "That felt so great out there. I love playing Hannah. I love this theater company." Her voice is quiet in the midst of all the chaos around us. Then she leans over and whacks my leg, the way she does to Gregor. "You better be coming to the party, Ellie, 'cause you're officially part of this company too."

Approval from Shantel. That's totally worth celebrating. "Try and stop me," I say.

Rachel leans over. "Me too?"

"Welcome to your dorm, baby," Shantel shouts.

Rachel wrinkles her nose. "I'm gonna take that as a yes."

*   *   *

"Shall we, Snow White?" Gregor says as he and I stand by the backstage door, ready to go outside. "Our fans await."

I take his arm. "You really don't need to call me Snow White anymore."

"Little Orphan Annie?"

"Really, really not!"

"Piper?"

"Tomorrow."

He opens his mouth, takes a deep breath. "*The sun will—*"

"You are *not* going to sing that song."

"Wow. So bossy. No wonder you make a good Piper."

"No wonder."

I push open the door.

"Omigod, omigod, Ellie, there you are! Congratulations! Oh, I missed you so much." Cassidy flings her arms around me and squeezes the ability to speak right out of me.

I hear Gregor greeting his family. "Grandma, Grandpa, you came."

Over Cassidy's shoulder, I spot her mom, holding a wrapped bouquet of flowers, standing next to Dad. They both sport smiles big enough to injure themselves.

"I can't believe you're here," I finally manage to say.

"Me neither." Cassidy lets me go. Her blue eyes shine. "That show was amazing. A-maz-ing! I'm so glad Mom had to come to town for her teacher conference thingy. As soon as she told me the date, I said, *Mom, you have to take me with you. I have to see Ellie's Toronto debut.*"

"I'm so glad she did," Mrs. Shannon says. "You were wonderful, Ellie. As always." She hands me the flowers. Just like she did for every show Cassidy and I did together.

"Thank you. I only wish you both could have seen one of the performances where I'm Piper. It's a bigger role. I mean," I say to Cassidy, "not Maria in *West Side Story* big, but—"

"Shut up!" Cassidy says, taking my hands in hers and shaking them. "Who cares? You were in a fantastic show in a fantastic theater with a fantastic cast in this crazy-big city. I'm so jealous. I'm so happy to see you."

How could I have already forgotten how funny and over-the-top sweet Cassidy is in person? I miss her all over again. "I'm so happy to see you too, Cass."

"Hey, can I get a hug?" Dad's still standing a little back from us.

I walk into his arms. "Thanks for coming, Dad."

"I'm so proud of you, kiddo. Great show."

"Thanks. And thanks for calling me that morning when you did the spot about YWTC. It got me to tonight."

"Just doing my job. Both jobs."

"Now, about that Renée," I say, leaning away. "Specifically, you and Renée."

He blushes, so I know I'm on to something. "That's a conversation for later," he says, then gestures to Cassidy, who's busy introducing herself to Gregor. "Do you want to have Cassidy sleep over at the condo? I asked her mom, and she said that'd be fine. They're at a hotel downtown until tomorrow."

"They're only here for one night? But there's a cast party." I look around. Some of the younger kids are leaving with family members, but the ones my age and older are hanging around with each other, probably sorting out how to get to Brayden's.

"It's up to you," Dad says.

The backstage door opens, and Marissa comes out alone. She scans the crowd and lights up, waving. "Mom, Dad, Daniel. Over here."

I dash over. "Can I grab you for just a second, Marissa? There's someone I want you to meet."

I half expect her to brush me off, but I suppose I've surprised her enough that she says, "Um, okay. Just a sec, you guys," she calls to her family.

I take her over to where Cassidy has now, by the looks of it, met Gregor's entire extended family.

"Ah, the Piper!" An elegant, silver-haired lady intercepts us when she spots Marissa.

"Both Pipers, Grandma," Gregor says. "When you come back tomorrow night, you'll get to watch the other one."

"Oh, good," she says, squeezing Marissa's and my hands. She has tangerine nails, multiple rings and a surprisingly strong grip. "My favorite character. So nasty. Those are the fun ones to play, right, girls?"

"Yes," Marissa and I both say.

"Grandma used to do plays when she was young," Gregor explains.

"I'm where Gregor gets his talent from." She winks and releases our hands. "Now. Where did your grandfather get to, Gregor? Oh, never mind, I found the old fool." She sets off to join a group that seems to make up half of the crowd outside.

"I should talk to my family," Marissa says.

"Right. I still haven't introduced you to who I want." The night is turning into a babbling, busy blur of people. "Cassidy, I want you to meet someone. Cassidy, Marissa. Marissa, Cassidy." It's like having my past meet my present.

"Marissa. You were so, so fantastic," Cassidy exclaims.

"Cassidy's my best friend from back in Rossmere Heights." For a frantic moment I try to remember if I ever texted anything horrible about Marissa to Cassidy, but I think I'm safe. Cassidy never asked for many details about my rehearsals. That's turned out to be a good thing. "She's only here for tonight."

Marissa gives Cassidy a genuine smile. "Oh, so you didn't get to see Ellie as Piper. That's too bad. She does a great job."

I stare at Marissa. "Thanks."

She turns to me. Shrugs. "It's true."

It's not exactly gushing praise, but from Marissa, I'll take it.

"Hey, Cassidy," she says as she starts to make her way to her family. "Since you're only here one night, you should go to the cast party. Brayden would love it."

"Yes!" Gregor shouts. "Brilliant idea."

"You're not going, Marissa?" I call.

"I'm tired. I think I still need to rest more after—" She mimes throwing up, laughs and gives a wave.

"Oh, I'd love to come," Cassidy bubbles beside me. "But. Well. I'm not part of the cast." She looks at me as if waiting for permission. After all of her texts about rehearsals in Rossmere, it's strange to realize I'm the one having the exciting time now. It's even better to realize I want to share it with her.

"Cassidy, do you know any show tunes?" Gregor asks in a life-or-death tone.

"Does she know show tunes?" I wrap my arm around Cassidy. "Us two and show tunes go way back."

"That settles that. She's coming," Gregor declares.

We sort out details with Dad and Mrs. Shannon about how we're getting to the party and when Dad will come pick us up. I hand him my bouquet for safe-keeping, and then Cassidy and I join Gregor and the others and head to the subway.

As we walk together, I watch Cassidy taking in the busy traffic, the people hurrying by on the sidewalk, the tall buildings all around us. A police car starts its siren, and she flinches. "Doesn't this city scare you sometimes?"

"It did," I admit. "But not anymore. Now it feels like home."

And that feels even better than the brightest spotlight ever could.

Acknowledgments

There are times when writing a book can be as nerve-racking as any opening night. Thanks to Pat Bourke, Karen Krossing, Karen Rankin and Erin Thomas for holding my hand through any jitters and helping me get my lines right. Thanks also to Sarah Harvey, Robin Stevenson and the entire Limelights team at Orca for bringing *Upstaged* into the (shared) spotlight. To David, Bronwyn and Caroline, thank you for always standing in the wings with your love and encouragement. And finally, a standing ovation to all the young musical-theater performers I know for showing me the joy—and, yes, the drama—that can come from hard work and singing at the top of your lungs in public places. Take a bow!

PATRICIA McCOWAN has been addicted to theater and books from a very young age. Her stories have appeared in YA anthologies and in print and online magazines. Her first novel, *Honeycomb*, was published in the Orca Limelights series. *Upstaged* is her second novel. For more information, visit patriciamccowan.com.

The following is an excerpt from
another exciting Orca Limelights novel
by Patricia McCowan.

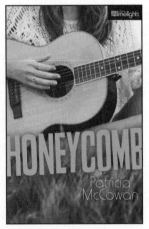

9781459805798 $9.95 PB
9781459805811 EPUB · 9781459805804 PDF

WHEN NAT, HER BEST FRIEND JESS and singing-star wannabe
Harper sing together, their harmonies bring down the house.
For Nat, the experience sparks a driving new desire to perform.
When the girls form a trio and enter a contest for a chance to play
at the Tall Grass Music Festival, Nat finds that harmony—musical
and otherwise—is hard to maintain.

One

I don't have butterflies in my stomach; I have big flapping pelicans. I've never been so nervous. In the dark backstage of an old church auditorium, Harper stands in front of me, watching the act that's before ours. She's pulled her dark, curly hair into a pile on top of her head, and excitement sparks off her like a meteor shower. Jess waits beside me, rock-steady as always, her guitar slung toward her back, her hands in her jeans pockets.

The three of us are the last act on the last day of March-break music camp, and I'm hoping the act onstage will never end. Not because five guys doing an all-horns version of "Smoke on the Water" is great. It's weird. But once Brassed-Off is done, we're up.

Why am I so nervous? I've sung in front of tons of people at school choir competitions. But it's easy to blend in with a choir. In three-part harmony, if I suck, I'll stand out. It's the standing out I'm afraid of.

Harper stage-whispers, "We are so gonna bring the house down after these goofs." She glances at me, winces, puts her hands on my cheeks. "Nat. Girlfriend. Breathe."

I take a deep breath.

"Now put your stage face on."

I do my best to smile as if I mean it. I can't let her and Jess down. "It's okay. I'm good."

"You're gonna be more than good, Nat. You're gonna be great. *We're* gonna be great." She puts her arm around my shoulders. I've known Harper only a week, but already she treats me like her best friend.

Still, I look to Jess—Jess and me and singing have gone together since grade one. "Harper's right," she says.

The pelicans in my stomach stop flapping so hard.

Applause. The Brassed-Off guys bow and come bouncing past us, high-fiving and fist-bumping one another. Harper rolls her eyes.

Darrell Bishop, the head of the camp, bounds out of the audience and onto the stage. The lights shine off his wire-framed glasses and perfectly bald head. "Was that not awesome?" he shouts. The audience claps.

He glances toward us, making sure we're ready. Jess pulls her guitar into position. Harper flashes a huge smile. She grabs my wrist and squeezes. I can't tell if it's to reassure me or to keep me from bolting.

Darrell gives us a thumbs-up and turns back to the audience. *Our* audience. "To finish off tonight's showcase of terrific young musicians, let's welcome to the stage three velvet-voiced gals. This trio couldn't agree on a name for their group"—the audience laughs, and Darrell raises one hand—"but that's okay, because they only came together this week, and hey, they sure find harmony when they sing. Ladies and gentlemen, I give you Harper Neale, Natalie Boychuk and Jess Lalonde."

Harper pulls me into the light. Jess follows close behind. Pelicans or not, it's time to sing.

Harper takes center stage behind the microphone, with me and Jess flanking her. We're tight together in a bright circle of light. It makes Jess's smooth black ponytail shine. Harper's caramel-colored skin seems to glow. I'm probably half-invisible beside them, all wispy blond hair and pale eyes.

Harper cozies up to the mic. "Fellow music geeks and gods," she starts, her voice silky, relaxed. At home. "I can't believe we've been together for only a week. It already feels...I don't know, like we're a family." She shades her eyes to look out at the other musicians, who have joined the audience. "Is that corny?"

"No!" they cheerfully yell.

Wow. Harper is only a year older than Jess and me—she's sixteen—but she can banter like a pro. Down in the front row, Darrell beams.

Harper smiles and nods. "Cool, cool. So, to keep this family-groove thing going, the girls and I have a song to share with you. Sound okay?"

The audience whistles and cheers. I quietly clear my throat and hope no one can hear my knees knocking together.

"Sweet," Harper says. She looks over to Jess, who smiles her easygoing smile as she strums the intro to "Four Strong Winds."